The Moments Between the Apocalypse

by Lina Hailings

Dedicated to J. You talked me into writing this, you're sharing the blame, you bastard.

Chapter One

There were a lot of things that frustrated me about the wizarding community, and chief among them was their strange isolationism, which resulted in them being at least 50 years behind the mortal world in terms of technology. Which meant that to research what I needed for the spell I was working on, I needed to find one book somewhere in the Prismatic Spire's innumerable libraries without so much as a search bar.

The library staff were usually friendly enough to ease that particular inconvenience, but today, they seemed awfully short-staffed, with lines forming for their aid. After a lengthy wait, the librarian aiding me was happy to inform me they had the book in stock. As I noted down where to find it, I quietly asked, "Is it just me, or are all the libraries running slow today?"

The librarian's face fell. "Haven't you heard? The master of tomes was replaced by a shapeshifting demon months ago, and it was only discovered the other day. There's chaos up and down the chain of command."

"Oh," was all I could manage to say. It wasn't the first I'd heard of the demons getting bolder of late, but until now, they hadn't struck such a high-ranking target, or one that affected me so directly. I struggled to process this as I wandered between the library's shelves. I eventually found the book I was looking for and plucked it off the shelf. I returned with it to one of the innumerable library desks, but I found myself struggling to concentrate. I found myself wondering, *What next?* Would the demons attack a member of my research cabal? A friend? A family member?

I found my mind groping for something I could do, some way I could solve this problem … and found nothing. At least, nothing I wasn't already doing. I was no battlemage; I was a research mage, working on developing new spells, none of which would be any use in a fight. I wasn't high-ranking, either. The only real help I could provide was by adding my voice in the Circle's labyrinthine politics.

The problem was that the Circle was over two millennia old. While it had actually adopted democracy pretty early, the modern Circle was mired in layers upon layers of awkwardly drawn electorates, archaic rules and deep-seated biases, which meant only so much got done—and the wizards of the Circle had only so much of a say in it anyway. I'd joined the only real populist party in the Circle, called the Green Hands, and given them at least some of my time and money. They promised more action against demon activity, but they were very much a minority. I tried to tell myself that that alone meant I was taking part, but it seemed so … small. What could one voice do against millennia of apathy?

I sighed, forced the thoughts out of my mind and got back to work. I couldn't donate money I hadn't earned.

Another Friday night, another moment to set aside my worries and enjoy myself. Unlike many of my fellow wizards, I preferred mortal entertainments to magical ones, specifically tabletop wargaming. I pulled a small trolley full of my models (created with magic—bloody expensive to just buy plastic!) towards the game store I played at.

I then found a logistical issue: the ramp that I normally pulled the trolley up was being repainted. There were stairs, but it wasn't a short flight, and I carried my models in a trolley because the large boxes of them were too heavy for me. I could carry the boxes one by one, but that would take time, and I wasn't eager to leave all of my things in the busy street.

As I was pondering the problem, one of the other wargamers approached.

Veronica Wainwright.

My crush.

She was seven feet of muscle, with broad shoulders and sharp features. Her tank top showed pale skin littered with both scars and tattoos; a deep slash here, a stylised wolf there. Her eyes were a clear blue, one of them framed by an old burn. Her ginger hair was shoulder-length, tied back in a ponytail. She was carrying her own set of boxes by hand.

"Hey, Sarah," she greeted me. As I tried to disengage from my fantasies of her pinning me to the ground in order to free up my brain to make conversation, she sized up the situation. "Need a hand?"

"Er, yes. Any ideas?" I asked.

Veronica set her boxes down on the trolley, on top of mine. Then, she lifted the entire thing. She carried all the boxes and the trolley up the entire flight of stairs without so much as a grunt of exertion. She set the trolley down at the top and turned to me. Seeing I was still at the bottom, gaping in awe at her feat of strength, she smirked. "Want me to carry you up too?"

The rational part of my mind told me that this was obviously a joke and that agreeing would have significant social—and potentially logistical—repercussions, but not before my love-struck dumb bitch of a self nodded enthusiastically. Just as I realised what I had done, but before I had the courage to try and laugh off my mistake, Veronica shrugged. She walked back down the stairs. Then, with one swift movement, she swept me up into a bridal carry.

My heart pounded as she causally carried me back up the stairs and carefully set me down alongside my belongings. I felt my face flush a deep red. Veronica simply grinned, retrieved her boxes and headed inside, leaving me to stare after her. When she left my line of sight, I realised what I was doing and hurried after her.

The night was just getting started. People were scattered around, busily setting up miniature battlefields and chatting about the games. I quickly pulled my trolley into the corner and found Veronica nearby (she was hard to miss). There was a lot I *wanted* to say to her, but how? And when? Our friendship seemed to be building steadily enough, but what happened next? Did Veronica even like me, or was she secretly annoyed by me and just humouring me? Honestly, was she even romantically interested in women?

But the idea that she might be interested, that she might one day kiss me, that she might grow to like picking me up and casually carrying me around—and, of course, with muscles that size? I doubt I weighed anything to her. She could cradle me like a baby in her arms. It was a fantasy I enjoyed far too much to just let go. Maybe I should just tell her how I feel. She could straight-up reject me, and I could get to work on moving on and forgetting about ——

"Want a game?"

Veronica's voice interrupted my train of thought. I decided actually addressing my feelings could wait another day (or week, or month, or year …) "Yeah, sure."

The two of us were a roughly even match, strategically. We both took a fair share of the other's models off the board, and both of us had to think. But an unlucky roll at a crucial moment lost me the game. The dice elicited a coarse word or two from me, but I was happy to wish Veronica a good game and accept her vice-like handshake.

The pair of us spent some time talking about the match, a conversation which then wandered to the game in more general terms. It was a subject I enjoyed; I'd spent a lot of time pondering both the game's rules and story, and I was eager to share my insights to whoever would listen, and listen Veronica did. After what could easily have been 10 minutes, I found myself finally out of breath. I then realised that Veronica had hardly said a word for … a while. I rubbed the back of my neck. "Uh, sorry. I kind of infodumped there, didn't I?"

Veronica smiled. "It's fine. Honestly, I like hearing you infodump."

I blushed.

A few days later, I was trying to beat some esoteric knowledge into my head when my phone buzzed. Eager for the distraction, I opened it to find a text from Veronica.

You free this afternoon? My gym partner called in sick and I could use someone to spot me.

Veronica, working out … and I didn't have anything on this afternoon.

Sure!

So, a couple of hours later, I was awkwardly entering a gym in the city, a pretty standard affair with various gym rats working out on colour-coordinated exercise machines. I felt pretty out-of-place, not owning much sportswear myself. Veronica was waiting for me in the lobby. She said something as I approached, but my brain decided it would much rather process the fact that she was wearing a sports bra and yoga pants. Her heavily built muscles were on full display, and I could see solid abs. I tuned back into the conversation in time to realise she was inviting me to store my things in the locker room and then get to work.

As she led me there, I noticed something a little odd: some kind of concave, detailed metal disc was embedded in her flesh, halfway between her chest and navel. I wasn't sure if it was appropriate to comment, but my curiosity overpowered my uncertainty. "Hey, Veronica. What's …" I gestured towards the implant.

Veronica glanced down at where I was pointing. "Oh, that? Experimental medical thingamajig. Some medical guys are trying to make new pacemakers. I signed up for a clinical trial. Not supposed to say much more."

Something about that didn't entirely add up in my mind, but medical history was a personal subject pretty much by definition, and I could think of a dozen good reasons why she might hold something back. It wasn't my business anyway, so I dropped the matter.

Soon enough, I was spotting Veronica as she bench-pressed so many weights I wasn't sure the bar would hold. Veronica held, though, and did so easily. She barely struggled, leaving little for me to do other than watch her mountain of muscles flex with each motion.

In-between sets, she was approached by a band of brawny men, wearing the short hair and clean faces usually indicative of soldiers. The one at the fore, a tanned man with a scar running across his lip, greeted her. "Hey, V. Who's this?"

Veronica seemed surprised to see them. "Oh, uh, you said —or I heard that you couldn't make it, so I asked her to spot me! Right, this is Sarah. She's from that wargaming group. Sarah, these are some friends from work: Jace, Harry, Cole and Kent."

The men briefly glanced at me as I waved awkwardly, before the one who had spoken first (now identified as Jace) looked back at Veronica. "Why'd you think that?"

Veronica shrugged noncommittally. "I heard. I guess we got our wires crossed somewhere."

The men furrowed their brows suspiciously. Veronica answered with a series of gestures that were clearly some kind of sign language or hand signal. It took her friends a moment to parse, but when they did, they laughed. Harry, a lithe but very athletic man of Asian ethnicity, said, "Alright, alright. Sure."

As they walked off towards the locker room, Cole, a stocky man down a few teeth, leaned towards me. "She once dropped a fart so bad the entire place thought we'd been hit with a chemical attack." He laughed again, giving a glaring Veronica a wicked grin. Veronica aimed an offensive gesture at him as he left.

I decided to not give Cole's story any consideration. Instead, I asked "Where *do* you work?"

"Private security group."

I glanced between her and her friends. "Makes sense. Honestly, I was expecting army. Not too far off."

Veronica idly ran a finger across one of her tattoos. "I mean, I used to be army. A lot of us were. Anyway …" Veronica shook her head, as if to shake off unpleasant memories.

We got back to work; or rather, she got back to work, and I happily watched.

Another of my mortal hobbies was tabletop roleplaying. I enjoyed the chance to take some time away from the misery of the real world and pretend to be a sci-fi assassin. I had also talked the girl running the group into inviting Veronica; I'd framed it by pointing out that larger groups were more stable, but honestly I just wanted to spend more time with her. It had turned out well, with Veronica actually having fun and contributing her fair share, even if she wasn't the most dedicated role-player.

This particular night, the group had decided we'd show up dressed as our characters. I was never a hand at the sewing machine, but I always had a knack for conjuration magic. So, I managed to conjure myself a skin-tight leather catsuit and a whole suite of straps and buckles. I sized myself up in the mirror. I was very short, with a body that seemed to have half-assed puberty.

Combined with my messy brown hair and green eyes, it made me pretty much the opposite of the tall, blonde bombshell that was my character. Still, the outfit was pretty flattering for what assets I did have, and I did feel kind of sexy. A little exposed, but just far enough out of my comfort zone that it was exciting rather than distressing.

En route to the house where we played, I encountered a minor problem, which came in the form of being dressed in a sexy costume in the middle of a bus interchange. I told myself that people in cosplay did this all the time, and there really wasn't all that much to worry about.

Then I saw the gaggle of men approaching me, leering. Most carried half-empty beer bottles, and they walked with the arrogant swagger of those who hadn't grasped the concept of actions having consequences. My heart raced; the interchange was busy at this time of day, and there was security everywhere, so I had reason to hope they wouldn't do anything extreme. Still, I wasn't dressed for them, and I wasn't totally naive. I walked closer to where one of the interchange workers was walking a crowd cross the street; with any luck, the authority and the people would discourage the men from doing anything worse than looking.

I was wrong.

One of them groped me.

All the initial attention meant I was already treading the thin line between excitement and distress, and this pushed me way across it. I shrieked, ineffectually slapping the hand away. The man and his gaggle of friends simply laughed, a few spouting lewd comments. A couple of people nearby glared at the men. A few walked up and started confronting them. But there were at least ten of them, all spoiling for a fight, and they simply brushed off anyone who approached them.

Until their leader bumped right into Veronica.

She was wearing a faux doctor's outfit, a fake lab coat with a blue cross stitched on it and a toy stethoscope. But it did little to hide her size or brawn. She glared at the man that had groped me. Clearly unused to any serious challenge, he slurred "What? She was asking for it!"

Veronica punched him so hard I saw a tooth fly out. He dropped like a sack of bricks, unconscious before he even hit the ground. The show of force gave the gaggle of other young men pause. One or two drew knives. The bystanders started calling for help, backing off from the armed men. Veronica was entirely unfazed. "What? He was asking for it."

I was relieved for a moment when a pair of policemen approached. Much less so when one, a tattooed man with incredibly over-styled facial hair, pulled his gun and pointed it right at Veronica's head. "On the ground! Now!"

I could see Veronica's muscles tense, like a snake coiling to strike, but she simply stared across the gun's sights to look the cop in the eye. "Tabby. Been a while. Want to kill civvies professionally?"

Some of the bystanders tried to explain what had happened to the police, but 'Tabby's' partner simply shoved them away. Tabby (the moniker was a little odd—his hair was brown, not ginger) tightened his grip on his pistol. "I said, on the ground!"

One of the brutish men was examining the one Veronica had punched. "Fuck, she broke his jaw!"

My heart raced. Veronica clearly had a history with Tabby, a none too pleasant one. And the cops were drunk on their own power, looking for an excuse to abuse it. There was no way Veronica would survive a point-blank shot, even with all her brawn.

But I had a trick or two up my sleeve. There was a lot that was fake about my outfit, but the innumerable pockets had room for a couple of spell reagents. I pulled a little magic from the surrounding æther, shaping it with my will. I grabbed a pinch of glitter, pulling the magic through it, letting the matter shape it like glass shapes light. With a subtle gesture, I pulled the magic into reality.

A small, mesmerising sparkle glimmered in my hand.

Tabby blinked. "Wha——"

I'd likened Veronica to a coiled snake, but the speed with which Veronica moved shamed their strike. She grabbed the slide of the pistol with one hand, and with the other, delivered a quick palm strike to the throat of the other cop. The tiny spell had already dissipated, but it had given Veronica the only chance she needed.

As Veronica and Tabby struggled over the gun, the assortment of thugs rushed to the fight. Seemingly with eyes in the back of her head, Veronica dodged each strike. While one hand controlled the gun, the other lashed towards the goons like arcing lightning, each strike eliciting screams of pain from Veronica's enemies.

One charged Veronica with a broken bottle. Suddenly changing the grapple like a wrestler, Veronica manoeuvred Tabby between her and the other attacker. The bottle was caught on Tabby's ballistic vest, but the impact caused him to lose his footing. Veronica took the chance to disarm him. With a spin, she knocked out another assailant and cleared herself of them for just a second. A second she spent ejecting the gun's magazine and clearing the chamber with the speed of a machine, before pegging it right at an attacker, nailing him on the nose with a wet crunch.

When the next thug threw a punch, Veronica grappled him, slamming him into one of his friends before kicking him back and using the inertia to twist his arm in a painful-looking way. Tabby pulled out a baton and rushed at Veronica. The cop was clearly much more practised in fighting than the drunk thugs, but Veronica was able to parry every strike, with time left over to dispatch the last of the goons that hadn't got the message.

Then, Tabby's partner recovered from the first hit. He fired a taser. It hit Veronica. She spasmed, but she was still in the fight. Pushing off the first of the two cops, she swung around to the second, pulling the taser dart out of her and throwing a punch in the same motion. The hit seemed to have sapped some of Veronica's strength and speed, allowing the cop to parry the strike.

Tabby returned to the fight, and it was Veronica versus the two cops. Stronger opponents than the random drunks, their strikes faster and more precise, but Veronica managed to handle both at once. In a whirlwind of fists, Veronica managed to stun one with a strike to the nose and knock out his partner with a series of jaw strikes, then she spun around with a roundhouse kick that finished the fight.

Panting with exertion, Veronica stepped over the cluster of unconscious and groaning bodies on the ground and approached me. "You alright?"

I was still processing everything that had just happened. I was certain that I was supposed to swoon dramatically, but I didn't actually know what 'swooning' actually meant. Instead, I just stammered "I … you … a … a little shaken, but alright." *Yeah, real damn cute, Sarah,* I thought sarcastically.

Veronica took off the lab coat and wrapped it around me. "Come on, let's grab a taxi."

The taxi ride was mostly quiet. Not being so exposed and being in a car with just a taxi driver and the woman who'd just saved me was comforting. As my heartbeat slowed, I began to process what Veronica had just pulled off. There had been at least a dozen opponents, two of them armed cops, and Veronica had beaten them single-handedly! To save *me!* I was already smitten, but this took it to a whole new level.

Halfway through the ride, Veronica received a phone call. "Hello? Oh, hey … Yeah, see, this asshole groped my friend, so I beat the crap out of him, but the cop … Yeah, but he and I, we knew each other from—well, can't say that on the phone. But he went straight for the gun. Look, what was I supposed to do? Let the guy walk? He sexually assaulted someone, for fuck's sake! Yeah … fine. Thanks." Veronica hung up, then turned to me. "My security group. Going to try to convince the cops that arresting me isn't worth the SWAT team they'd need to do it."

I wondered what kind of leverage this 'security group' had that they could do that (*maybe it did some embarrassing work for the government?*) but Veronica seemed to believe what she was saying, so I didn't comment further.

After we'd been dropped off in front of our destination, I quietly said to Veronica, "Thanks, by the way."

Veronica shrugged. "Don't mention it. Assholes had it coming."

As we approached the door, I asked "Er, 'Tabby'?"

Veronica had been about to knock, but she lowered her hand. "Yeah, Tabby." She sighed. "I'm under orders to not talk about this, but … I don't care much for those assholes, so I'll bend the rules a little. You kind of deserve to know." She turned to me, folding her arms. "I've mentioned I'm ex-army? Well, I was more than that. I was special forces."

My eyes widened. I couldn't deny it—I found badassness *incredibly* sexy. "Really!? I mean, I suppose that's how you, you know …"

Veronica smirked. "Learned how to beat the shit out of a whole bunch of assholes? Yeah. But Tabby, his real name's Kyle. He was part of my unit. Short version, he once boasted he was a tiger, someone else said he was more a tabby cat, and it stuck. Anyway … look, I'd better not say where and when. But we were sent to take out some insurgents holed up in a village. The villagers weren't exactly happy to see us, and honestly, due to a whole bunch of shit going on at the time, I didn't exactly blame them. But I figured hey, they send in spec ops to be precise, we wouldn't have to more than inconvenience them." Her shoulders slumped. "My CO disagreed."

"What happened?" I whispered.

"He planned…" Veronica's fists clenched in anger. "There was a lot of shit I was willing to do. The insurgents weren't nice people, and I'm not a saint either. But I don't gun down innocent civilians. Not … not children. I told him that. He said he'd given me an order. I punched that son of a bitch in his bitch-ass face."

I laughed quietly, though I was unsure whether it was from humour or nerves. "He deserved it."

Veronica hung her head. "The rest of the unit disagreed. They—look, I'm good, but not a-whole-platoon-of-spec-ops good. At least, I wasn't back then. So they beat me, tied me to a tree, and I watched as they …"

My heart sank. "Holy shit."

Veronica continued "The whole thing was hushed up. My unit got medals. I got a dishonourable discharge. Probably would have thrown me in jail if it hadn't meant they'd risk the whole thing being blown open in court."

I yearned to help her, to ease her heart—to *do something.* But what could I do? I felt helpless. "Look, you did the right thing. A lot more than most would have done."

Veronica looked distant. "Didn't amount to much."

I shook my head. "Not the point. You stood up to him. That needs to happen more often. And besides …" I smiled shyly. "You're my hero. You stood up to those goons just a few minutes ago, right? Even a couple of cops."

Veronica slowly smiled. "Thanks. That means a lot to me."

Veronica knocked, and we were greeted by the rest of our group, all of whom were surprised to see us. Apparently, the brawl at the interchange had already made headlines. As Veronica was insisting we could still play the game, she got another call. After she thanked whoever was on the other end, she assured us the rest of her firm had saved her from jail time. I got the impression she was up for a tongue-lashing from her superiors, but considering what had just happened, that wasn't such a bad ending.

The game was only mildly overshadowed by the fact that Veronica had just beat the crap out of a dozen dudes and shaken off being tazed. But as I waited between combat turns, an idea took root in my mind and began to sprout.

As the game wrapped up for the night, I spoke to Veronica. "Hey, Veronica? Look, I don't want a repeat of what happened at the interchange, so I was wondering if … you could take me home?" I lowered my shoulders, held my hands behind my back and tilted my head slightly in an effort to make myself look as small and protectable as possible.

It must have worked. "Yeah, sure."

So, Veronica joined me in moving from bus to bus on my way home. I stuck close to her and kept wearing the coat, which seemed to dissuade any further jerks from trying anything. I made it home without further incident. As we approached the door to my apartment block, I gave Veronica my best 'cute and innocent' look. "Do you want to come in?"

To my surprise, nothing was going wrong with the plan. "Sure."

I led her into my flat. Fortunately, I'd had the foresight to keep the bulk of my magical things tidied away in boxes or drawers when not in use, and much of what was left was hard to distinguish from the fine layer of clutter throughout the flat. It was at this point I uncovered a massive blank space in my planning: what happened next? Just start making out on my couch?

As I pondered the dilemma, Veronica said "So … that's a pretty tricky outfit you've got there. Need any help getting out of it?"

"Oh, it's really not that hard. Thanks anyway," I said awkwardly.

Veronica seemed disappointed. "Ah. Well, I won't intrude any further. G'night, Sarah." She left as I tried, and failed, to find some reason for her to stay.

I had settled into my pyjamas by the time I realised what Veronica had *actually* meant by helping me 'get out of' my outfit. I rushed over to my phone and called her, making sure not to give myself any time to rethink it. My heart pounded as I heard the phone ring.

Ring … (Am I really doing this?)

Ring … (Maybe I'm reading too much ——)

Click. "Veronica Wainwright."

"Er, hi, it's me. When you offered to help me, uh, you know, 'get out of my costume'. Um, were you … ?"

Veronica finished for me. "Flirting? Yeah. But look, if you're not interested ——"

"No, no! I—I'm just a *fucking* idiot."

Veronica sounded like she was trying, and failing, to keep the amusement out of her voice. "Did you really not … ? When you invited me inside, I kind of figured you wanted to, you know …"

I flung myself back on my bed. "No, I … I just …" I swallowed. "I really like you, Veronica. A lot. And, well, I was so caught up in the moment I honestly didn't think about what came next."

I could hear the smile in Veronica's voice. "Look, I'm on the bus right now, but if you're thinking about that, and feeling a little cold tonight …"

This time, I picked up on the euphemism, but the night's earlier events had tested my boundaries more than enough for one night. "Um, if you're talking about—look, after earlier, I'm not feeling like going much further tonight. But I really like you, Veronica. A lot. So if, um … you wanted to, you know, grab dinner or something?" I squirmed anxiously.

"Sure."

Chapter Two

A date. With Veronica. The woman who had pretty much saved my life. I hadn't been on a date since high school, and that was a disaster borne of my attempts to convince myself I was straight. Alright, so I would settle on something classic. Dinner, maybe a movie. But where? Or would Veronica choose something? I certainly should pick up the bill, it would be the least I could do after——

"Sarah? Sarah!"

One of my colleagues, a tall woman with a bad case of resting bitch face called Janet, pulled me back to the present. I was in the middle of an arcane laboratory, working with some colleagues on studying the properties of a new rune. "Hm? Oh, sorry, I was—anyway, you were saying?"

She tapped a sketch on the nearby blackboard. "Do you have any thoughts?"

I looked at the blackboard, trying to recall what she had said in the past few minutes. "Uh … about what?"

Another of my colleagues, a round and bearded man named Will, glared. "About whether or not we should try inscribing the rune in silver or copper next!"

I quickly assessed the issue. "Well, silver's a bit more expensive, and our budget comes back through in November, right?"

Will said, "That's what I just said!"

I squirmed. "Sorry, sorry, I'm just distracted."

Janet sighed. "Yeah, I know. I've been trying not to think about the demons myself, but …"

I flushed. "It's not that, I just—I have a date. In a few days."

Will's eyes widened. "What?"

I hurried to explain myself. "I haven't been on a date since high school! I'm not sure if I have anything to wear, and honestly, I'm worried I'll mess it up! She's just *her*, and I have no idea what she sees in me! She ——"

Janet interrupted, "Sarah!" She tapped on the blackboard. "We're supposed to be studying magic?"

"Sorry, sorry. Okay, can we take it from the top?"

Veronica had chosen a bar she knew: a relatively up-scale but not overly expensive place, or so she had promised. I had absolutely no idea what to wear, and I couldn't decide until the day, which I spent rushing a conjuration spell to assemble a simple black dress. I was halfway through putting on my make-up when she knocked. I hurriedly called "Sorry, still getting ready! Just give me five minutes!"

After I took 10, I sheepishly opened the door to find Veronica standing in a simple but nice dress shirt and pants. I hurried to apologise. "Sorry, sorry! I completely lost track of time!"

Veronica shrugged. "No problem. You look good."

"You too!" I managed to squeak. Gods, we hadn't even left my place and this was already going awfully. I tried making some small talk as we left, but I was stammering and stumbling over my words. What was I even doing? Veronica was way too good for a socially inept half-mage like me.

Veronica led me to an older bar on the edge of the city, with no mobs of drunken just-barely-not-teenagers or throbbing music. While we were looking at the menu, I found a solution to my racing heart: alcohol. I didn't drink often, but what harm could a little liquid courage do?

As soon as the drink arrived, I downed almost half of it. Veronica raised an eyebrow. I flushed. "I'm sorry. I'm just nervous."

Veronica laughed. "There's no need to be nervous! I like spending time with you."

I squirmed from the praise. Dammit, how long did alcohol take to kick in? "I—really? I just … um, I mean ——" I proceeded to chug the rest of my drink.

Veronica laughed. "Never pegged you as the heavy drinker."

"I-I'm not. I just. *I'm nervous.* You're just so—so *you*! And I don't want to fuck this up. You're not like anyone I've ever met. You saved my life! You're my knight in shining armour! And you're so big, and strong, and you carried me that one time! Literally! And I just … you're supposed to feel smarter when you're drunk, right? Maybe I need to be more drunk." I flagged down a passing waiter for a drink.

> …
>
> …
>
> …

I was barely conscious and already regretting the previous night. My head pounded from the hangover. I tried to remember what exactly had happened, but even the slightest effort of recollection was unbearably difficult. I groaned in pain.

It was then that I felt someone gently stroke my hair, and I realised I was lying on the chest of (presumably) that same someone. I was too hungover to even move, but I could faintly catch Veronica's scent. She was pretty comfortable, all things considered. I also realised I was in my underwear. My brain certainly had lost too many cells to process the implications of that. I elected to simply remain still for the time being; my headache was a compelling suggestion against doing anything at all.

Then there was either a blaring alarm, or a phone notification, I was too hungover to tell the difference. I felt Veronica move, heard the alarm silence, followed by Veronica saying, "Someone better be dying." This was followed by an "Ah, shit." in a tone that made me suspect someone was, in fact, dying. I felt myself being lifted slightly into the air as Veronica manoeuvred herself out from under me, then I was laid gently back onto the couch (couch? I was expecting my bed) as, to my surprise, Veronica gently kissed me on the forehead. Then, I heard Veronica hurriedly getting dressed and leaving.

I lay there for a while, unmoving. Eventually, my hangover had faded enough for me to sit up. I sifted through what little I could recall of the previous night. I was nervous. I tried to drown my nerves with drink … *ugh, what was I thinking!?* I knew damn well that that could have backfired in a dozen ways, and it had in at least one. I buried my head in my hands. Gods, what did I say to Veronica?

I managed to wake myself up enough to get some water, and then some breakfast. All the time, I started to piece together the implications of what little I could recall. I wasn't the most eloquent at the best of times, and last night I'd had more drinks than I'd ever had in my life.

There was also the matter of my dress. The conjuration spell was hasty and cheap, so there was no chance it would have survived the whole night. That, at least, explained why I had woken up in my underwear. But what would Veronica have seen? I doubted she was aware of the supernatural.

Eventually, I realised there was only one way to get any solid answers to those questions: call Veronica. I dialled her number. My tension rose with every ring, until…

"The person you are trying to call is not available. Please leave a message after the tone." *Beep.*

"Erm, hi, Veronica? It's Sarah. I just wanted to talk about what happened last night. If you could call me back …" Not sure how to end the message, I trailed off awkwardly then hung up. I cursed. Hardly anyone's fault, but it was a conversation I'd rather have sooner than later.

Having little to do that day, I managed to change into some pyjamas before lying on the bed, my phone on the bedside table. I simply stared at it, waiting for it to ring. Waiting. Waiting.

Minutes turned to hours. Eventually, I convinced myself to get up and grab some lunch, keeping my phone close at hand. I tired of the tension, but I couldn't bring myself to relax. For a while, it remained likely that Veronica was simply too busy to answer, but as midday faded to afternoon, the chance steadily waned. The idea that Veronica didn't want to talk to me took root.

My thoughts were interrupted by a tapping on the balcony door. I turned to find a messenger bird, a drab grey thing commonly summoned by wizards that hadn't yet figured out how to text. I opened my balcony door, and it flew inside, depositing a note at my feet before disappearing into the æther. The note was signed by Janet.

Sarah,

Janet

I collapsed onto my couch. As if I needed something else to worry about. Magical research wasn't exactly a fun hobby, but I was proud of my work; I'd certainly put a lot in. Being set back was a bitter thought, and not knowing by how much somehow only made matters worse. What was worst of all was how damn *powerless* I felt. Not all that different from the situation with Veronica, in truth. In both cases, all I could really do was lie down and worry.

As afternoon faded into evening, I managed to dig myself out of the hole of misery and got to doing something with myself, but both matters weighed heavily on my mind.

I didn't hear from Veronica for days. How badly had I screwed up? Then, the night of the roleplaying group came around again. My anxiety was building; would Veronica be there? Would she want to speak to me? What would she even say? Would she call me out for getting drunk in front of the rest of the group?

I arrived at the place and knocked nervously. The door opened, revealing the group's GM, a bubbly woman named Abby with generous amounts of fat. "Hey Sarah!"

"Erm, hi. Is—is Veronica here yet?" I stammered.

Abby looked a touch concerned. "Yeah. Is something wrong?"

I gulped. "I just need to talk to her."

Abby led me into the lounge, where I found Veronica watching TV. She looked up as I entered and smiled. "Sarah! I've been meaning to text you, but my phone was destroyed."

I sighed in relief. "Oh! Oh. It's just—I'm an idiot. I didn't hear back from you, and in my head I turned it into this big thing. Can we talk?"

Veronica stood. "Sure."

I led her to the house's backyard for a measure of privacy. I decided I should start. "I should apologise for how I acted the other night."

Veronica chuckled. "It's fine. Honestly, kind of impressive how you managed to get absolutely smashed off two drinks."

I flushed. "I-I normally don't drink. I was just so nervous."

"Yeah, you said so. Before saying some *very* flattering things about me."

My face must have been bright red. "Truth be told, I don't really remember much about the other night."

"Well, not much more to tell, actually." Veronica's stance turned a touch bashful. A strange look came over her. "You spent a lot of time explaining, well, how much you liked me. Caught me a little off guard, honestly. I didn't realise … anyway, after a while you started trying to take off your dress. I figured then that it was time to take you home."

Oh gods, no! The typical wizard approach of isolating oneself from mortal affairs was starting to look appealing.

Veronica reached for her wallet. "That reminds me, I probably owe you for the dress. When we got back to your place, I tried to get you into something more comfortable—not a euphemism—but, well, I guess I don't know my own strength."

Ah. The hasty mess of conjuration wasn't exactly structurally sound fresh from the æther; after a few hours, its integrity would be reduced to that of tissue paper. "Oh! Er, no need to worry. It was cheap anyway. My fault. I spent so long worrying about the date that I forgot I had nothing to wear, so I grabbed something that looked kind of good … it's my fault for leaving it so late."

Veronica returned her wallet to her pocket. "Alright then. Anyway, I tried tucking you into bed before getting some sleep on your couch, but you crawled on top of me saying nice things about my chest before you passed out."

I hung my head. "Sorry."

Veronica gently tilted my head back up so that I was looking her in the eye. "Nothing to apologise for. The whole thing was actually kind of cute. But you don't have to be so nervous. I like you. You're adorable, especially when you start talking about things you like. Or when you blush—just like that."

I squirmed awkwardly. "I … okay. Do you want to try again?"

Veronica nodded. "Sure. Let's go somewhere with less alcohol this time."

"Um, okay, what about …" *Alright, stay calm, what are places people go together?* "Uh, the zoo, maybe?"

"Can't do that, I've got a lifetime ban. Got into a fistfight with a gorilla. Long story." At the look I gave her, she added, "I won, for the record."

I was running through other possible destinations when Veronica kissed me. On the lips. It was short, just a quick peck, but it completely short-circuited my thinking. She smiled and walked back inside.

That date, a more relaxed affair in a cafe one morning, actually went well. It was a little awkward talking about myself when I couldn't exactly explain that I was a wizard, and Veronica couldn't say much about her private security firm, but we both had plenty in common; shared interests in wargaming and roleplaying, and a few movies and video games. We bounced from subject to subject and enjoyed each other's company.

A couple of nights later was wargaming night, and I was eager to show. I was late. Knowing Veronica would be there meant I spent way too much time working on my outfit. When I arrived, I found her already in a game, but she looked up and greeted me with a wide smile.

After I deposited my models, I walked up beside her and examined the board; she was winning pretty soundly. As I thought of a suitable comment, Veronica kissed me on the forehead (she was so tall, she had to bend down a little to do so). I blushed. Her opponent briefly raised their eyebrows but dismissed the matter with a shrug before rolling some more dice and wiping one of Veronica's units off the board.

I reminded myself that this wasn't a date and got to actually talking with *other* people, even played a game or two. Still, when it was time to go home, I wasn't complaining when Veronica approached me. "Hey, you doing anything else tonight? I was just thinking maybe we could grab some dessert."

I grinned. "Sure!" It was late at night, but it wasn't like anyone could threaten me with Veronica around.

The only place still open was a fast-food joint, but the mediocrity of the dessert was entirely offset but the fact I got to spend more time with Veronica. After we finished and headed to the bus interchange, she said, "So, it's pretty late. Want me to take you home?" Then, she leaned in and whispered, "If you want, I can see how hard *that* outfit is to get out of, if you know what I mean."

My heart raced. "Y-yeah, that'd be nice."

I held Veronica's hand most of the way home. On the bus, I nestled in closer to her, revelling in the physical contact. Veronica smiled and wrapped an arm around me, holding me. I looked up, doe-eyed, at her and came far closer than I'd like to admit to missing our stop.

When we reached my apartment, Veronica outright picked me up and carried me up the stairs. I giggled in elation, managing to unlock my apartment without her having to set me down. She carried me to the bedroom.

Somewhat to my surprise, I was the first to wake up in the morning. It was an enjoyable experience, being wrapped safe and sound in Veronica's heavily built arms. I snuggled deeper into her and decided to go back to sleep, basking in her warmth. I was woken sometime later by Veronica stirring. She held me a little closer, kissing me on the forehead.

She shifted slightly, rolling onto her back. One slight disadvantage to her massive frame was that she took up the bulk of the bed, though that was thankfully mitigated somewhat by my own small size. She sat up slightly. I came to the terrifying realisation that she wasn't about to cuddle. That simply would not do. I rolled over, shifting myself on top of her, and wrapped my arms around her. I took a moment to look up at her with a smile, meeting an expression that was a mix of surprise, confusion and affection, before I nestled as close as I could into her, holding her tight. I wrapped myself around her as much as I could, doing my best to return the affection.

After a pause, Veronica began to stroke my hair softly. Then, I heard something like a choked-back sob. I quickly looked up. "Is something wrong?"

Veronica looked emotional, but by her smile it seemed to be, mostly at least, positive emotions. "No, no, I just …" she seemed to be finding a way to express all her emotions. All she managed was, "You're real cute like that, you know?"

I smiled and nestled back into her.

A few nights later, there was another roleplaying night. Our characters had gotten themselves into some hot water, and the dice were rolling. I winced as my character got into hand-to-hand with a particularly large robot; not something that would end well. Abby turned to another member of the group, a scrawny man half-committed to a goth phase named Ryan, who was playing the group's hacker. "Your turn."

Ryan blinked; his thoughts were evidently elsewhere. "Hm? Oh, alright, I shoot them."

As he gathered up the dice, I snapped, "Er, hello? Giant robot kicking my ass?" I knew that his character could disable the thing remotely.

Ryan looked between me and Abby. "Wha——?"

Abby frowned. "Haven't you been paying attention?"

Ryan rubbed his eyes. "Sorry, it's—I spent all night at the club. Still a little tired."

It was a throwaway line. I couldn't shake the feeling that Ryan was hiding something. Meanwhile, another group member, a bearded brunet with plenty of bulk named Pat, frowned. "Club? Since when do you go to clubs?"

Ryan smiled, though I noticed his gaze seemed a little distant. "Oh, my mate Jason recommended it. It was great. I even got into the VIP section!"

Abby blinked. "How the hell did you manage that?"

"I—er, think I've said too much." Ryan seemed to shake off his thoughts, though he visibly deflated as he did so. "Right, hacking robots."

The rest of the game proceeded more-or-less normally, and Ryan was quick to leave after it wrapped up. Before the rest of us left, Abby said, "Is it just me, or was Ryan acting a little strangely?"

Pat nodded grimly. "Not just you. He's been acting odd all week. Blew off guitar practice two weeks in a row. And honestly, he's been … sick, I think. Worryingly pale, but he insists he's fine."

The first points of a disturbing pattern started to take shape in my mind. "When did he start going to that club?"

Pat got out his phone, checking Ryan's social media. "About two weeks ago."

Abby sighed. "I can't exactly stop him from going, can I?"

Pat started to pace the room anxiously. "He starts acting all distracted just after he starts going somewhere shady?"

Abby threw her hands up in the air. "Well, what are we supposed to do!? Even if you're right, we can't actually stop him!"

Pat stepped towards her. "I'll try! I have to do something! He's my friend!" After a pause, he added, "I'll check out the club next time he goes. Call the police if there's anything illegal going on."

Veronica looked deep in thought. "Dangerous."

Pat snapped, "Well, what's your idea?"

Veronica thought a while. "I'm going with you."

As the argument progressed, I considered a far more worrying possibility: a vampire. A friend becoming weirdly pale and obsessed with a night-based business … there *were* mundane explanations for that. But nightclubs were a vampire's favourite haunt; booming at night, with plenty of young patrons to prey on, and the kind of place where it wouldn't raise a fuss if someone decided to 'stay the night'. I cursed myself for not thinking to check Ryan for bite marks.

If that was true … Veronica was a dangerous woman, I'd learned that by now, but a vampire could easily catch any mundane soldier off guard. They had superhuman strength and speed, and they could develop a suite of dangerous occult powers. Worse, they could regenerate from any injury, save the burning light of the sun or a stake through the heart (and then, only if the stake stayed in). If Veronica wasn't ready for that … I mustered my courage. "I might go too. Just because I might get another chance to see Veronica be badass."

Veronica laughed.

Chapter Three

Going headfirst into what was *at best* a shady nightclub, and very possibly a vampire den—Gods, what was I thinking? But Ryan needed help, and I wasn't about to back down on my word. But I was careful to prepare. After the bus-stop brawl, I'd started work on a ring with a danger-sensing charm, and now was the perfect time to put it through its paces. I inscribed a bracelet with a basic protective charm, and my handbag was filled with spell components. I also brought a spray bottle full of water and powdered garlic. Like many things, the legends were half-right about garlic and vampires: they had no supernatural aversion to it, but it wreaked havoc on their supernatural senses, enough to buy a victim a few precious seconds. I revised my spell book, memorising a few spells that would help Pat, Veronica and I make a quick escape if one was needed. None of them were aware of the supernatural, but giving them that particular shock would be worth us not getting killed.

A couple of nights later, Pat picked the three of us up, and we went to the address he'd pulled from Ryan's phone (how exactly he did that, I elected to not ask). We found it in the middle of what were mostly office high-rises. There were no signs leading to the place, but I could hear the thumping of club music. I was already hating the place.

We got out of Pat's car and walked towards the noise. All of the buildings were locked up, but we found an alley, where a burly bouncer (though not *Veronica* burly) was guarding a side door. Before I could think of a plan, Pat walked straight up to him. "Is this the VIP entrance?"

The bouncer frowned. "If you were allowed in, you'd know that."

Veronica simply glared at the bouncer, pushing him aside and opening the door. She fixed him with a threatening gaze as Pat and I moved past the pair and headed inside. I was surprised to be met with the faint smell of chlorine. Veronica bringing up the rear, we followed a small corridor into what looked like a bathhouse, with low lighting and ever-present rhythmic music and various aesthetically pleasing folk in swimwear offering bottles of wine to a number of people of much more varied attractiveness.

I could see Veronica scanning the area, hand on a pocket of her cargo pants. Did I see the faint outline of a knife? Pat, meanwhile, hailed one of the servers. "Hey, I'm looking for Ryan. Lanky, kind of a goth guy?"

The server, a musclebound man with not a speck of body hair, said, "If he's not here or out front, he's with the boss upstairs."

Pat nodded. "Thanks."

I kept looking around as Pat navigated the corridors and staircases. I saw more than one goon in a suit staring right at the three of us, talking into a radio. Still, we were unchallenged as we walked into one of the club's upper levels, a balcony overlooking the bathhouse with a dancefloor visible through a window. There were various people lounging there, all young and attractive, but most had their attention on a thirty-something man in a fine suit in the centre, holding a glass of wine in his hand. Ryan was there, head resting on the man's shoulders.

A pair of bleeding wounds marked his wrist.

Pat's eyes were wide. "Ryan? Who's this?"

Ryan had a vacant and dreamy expression. "This … Mister Orden."

Mister Orden smirked. "And introduce me to your friends, my dear."

As Ryan dazedly told Orden our names, I glanced at the entrance we came through to see four guards approaching. I kept a hand in my bag. "We've got company."

Orden simply laughed. "Please, Miss Sarah, they're with me. I'm sure we can be civil here; a friend of Ryan is a friend of mine."

Pat widened his stance. "What the hell are you doing to Ryan?"

Orden laughed. "I'm just giving him new experiences! It's … hard to explain. Why don't I just show you?"

As Orden stood, I pulled out my spray bottle, blasting him in the face with garlic water. Orden gagged. "Ack! Bitch! Ugh!"

Yep. Vampire. "Ryan, we need to leave, now."

Orden glared at us, his eyes glowing a deep red. "Hold them!"

A trio of guards approached us, trying to grapple us. One pinned me easily. A second struggled a bit with Pat. The third Veronica punched straight in the solar plexus, before she pulled his gun and shot the guards who were after Pat and I dead.

I couldn't hear through the ringing in my ears, but I saw Orden growl and turn into a shadowy mist. Guessing his next move, I looked at Veronica. As expected, Orden materialised behind her. I went to shout a warning, but Veronica had obviously guessed the move as well, spinning around in a moment and landing a strike straight to Orden's neck. A sickening crack accompanied the strike, and the vampire's head twisted in an awkward way. As he stumbled back, Veronica flowed into a roll, evading more gunfire from Orden's guards and returning it with lethal accuracy.

My mind shoved the implications of the situation to one side; we were in a fight, and I had to do what I could to get us out alive (granted, the former special forces soldier didn't seem to need all that much help, but I wasn't taking chances). I reached into my bag of spell components, summoning mana with my will and shaping it with my mind. I pulled my hand from my bag, shouting an invocation, and a blast of wind sent another band of guards stumbling back. Not the most dangerous attack, but it kept them down for a few precious seconds. With how fast Veronica was moving, I doubt she needed any more.

Orden's other 'guests', Ryan included, cried in rage, charging Veronica. Just like at the bus interchange, Veronica turned into a whirlwind of movement, beating them all back easily. Pat grabbed on to Ryan, holding him back. "Ryan, the fuck are you doing!?"

I rushed up to the wrestling pair. "He's enthralled! Hold him still!" As Pat threw him into a pin, I drew some powdered silk from my bag, drawing it on Ryan's wrists and ankles in arcane patterns. With my will, bindings flashed into existence.

As Pat blinked at me, I felt my danger-sense ring thrum. Reflexively, I pumped my warding bracelet full of mana. A shield formed around me, absorbing a pair of bullets that would have killed me. The impact knocked me sprawling. The gunfire drew attention to another pair of guards that I saw just before Veronica shot them dead as well.

Orden growled in anger as he righted the position of his head and sprinted at Veronica. His speed was inhuman. Veronica was just as fast. She parried his strike, put the pistol to his chest and pulled the trigger. A human would be dead before they hit the ground, and even the vampire stumbled back, his inhuman physiology still struggling with such a wound.

As Pat ran up to me, I said, "I'm fine, I'm fine! We need to hold them!"

Pat clearly had no damn idea what was going on, but he trusted me enough to pin some of the thralls Veronica hadn't knocked out while I bound them with magic. Orden, meanwhile, took the chance to get back to his feet and fled up some stairs. Veronica hissed, rushing to where some of the guards lay dead. She took a gun from one, a couple of magazines from another. She looked at us. "Come on, let's finish this." She advanced up the stairs, gun raised. Deciding it was safest to be near the friendly ex-spec-ops, Pat and I followed, the former briefly stopping to acquire a gun himself.

On the staircase, we were confronted by a band of nightmarish, pale humanoids with elongated features and maws full of fangs: ghouls. Veronica gunned down the first two to attack, decked a third, ducked a strike from a fourth, shot that one in the head, followed by a fifth, then broke the neck of the third with a clean stomp. She kept advancing up the stairs.

We reached a series of walkways overlooking the more public areas of the club, where Veronica ducked back behind the stairs just in time for a few bullets to whizz past where her head had just been. Entirely unperturbed, she poked her head back up to return fire before advancing further. The next wave of attackers was revealed to be a pair of vampires, young (not that it was easy to tell, with the undead) things in leather jackets and armed with pistols. One was still reeling from the bullets Veronica had put in her. The other seemed to think his chances would be better in melee, and he charged. Veronica grappled him, using the momentum of the charge to fling the vampire into the lights above the club, the impact causing heavy damage to both, before the vampire took what had to be a two-storey fall onto the dance floor. Veronica immediately turned to the other vampire, putting a few more bullets in her.

Across the walkway, a door opened, and Orden, flanked by a pair of guards, sent a veritable storm of bullets towards Veronica. She ducked behind a pillar, reloading her gun. Pat and I ducked back behind the stairs, glancing at each other. Pat was panting breathlessly. "Okay, so how do you kill a vampire?"

I explained, "Burn them to ash. A stake through the heart keeps them down. Then you just put them somewhere sunny. Hold on." I pulled out a nail and carved some runes into the nearby wall. Most wizards wouldn't try conjuring solid objects on the fly, but a stake like the one we'd need was a very simple object, and I was pretty good at this. I managed to pull one into existence in under a minute—not the sturdiest or nicest-looking thing, but it would keep a vampire down for a few minutes.

Veronica, meanwhile, changed her approach. Using the railings for cover, she rolled towards a nearby wall, from which she vaulted onto some catwalks hanging from the club's roof. Rushing across them, she leapt, gunning down Orden's guards as she did so. She collided with Orden, knocking him down. The vampire threw her off and lunged. He managed to push Veronica's gun away, but Veronica simply responded by landing a headbutt straight on his nose. As he recoiled, she followed up by grabbing his head and driving it through a nearby desk. She took a splinter of wood from the remains and drove it straight through his heart.

The vampire still on the walkway had managed to stand at this point. Pat, seeing this, unloaded the gun he had taken at her. Normally, a single, untrained human couldn't do much against a vampire, but this one had been very much softened up by Veronica's previous attentions and didn't even realise she was under attack until more bullets started landing in her. They knocked her back down, and I took the chance to approach and push my own stake in.

Veronica walked up to me, still scanning the walkways. "Think that's the last of them."

Pat approached the vampire and shot her a few more times before the gun tumbled out of his hands. "Vampires … fucking … vampires."

Veronica pulled out her phone and dialled. "Access code, Wainwright 362 Falling Osprey. Get me ops … Yeah, it's me. Vampire den, need a cleanup. Three vampires, two staked, one …" She peered over the railing. "… unaccounted for. I'll sweep the area. Whole bunch of thralls, most of them tied up. Some shooters slotted. Yeah, thanks. See you soon." She hung up. Seeing the looks on our faces, Veronica explained to Pat and I, "I'm a monster hunter. Professional. My outfit are sending some backup to tidy up this mess. Going to go see if I can find that third vampire."

I crouched down by the freshly staked vampire. "I'll shore up the conjuration here, make sure it lasts. Wait, quicker solution." I hurried over to the ruined desk, glancing around in case there was any more danger. Seeing none, I took another fragment of wood from the remains and headed back to the vampire. I winced as a splinter or two found its way into me as I drove it in beside the conjured stake.

Veronica had headed back down to the club's lower levels, but Pat was standing still, clearly coming down off what was likely enough adrenaline to kickstart the heart of a whale. "He … and you … and she …"

I sat down, coming down off a rush myself. "Yeah, I'm a wizard. If you've got questions, I'll answer. Best I can."

Pat started with something simple. "Ryan …?"

"He'll … probably be alright. Reason to hope. Vampires, when they bite someone, turns them into a thrall. Basically mind control. Not healthy, but not a full vampire. Vampires use them as minions for things that need to be done during the day and don't need all that much skill. But you can recover if you go long enough without being bit. Once the vampire's out of the way, Ryan … next week or two might be rough for him, but he should recover." Pat nodded, sitting down beside me. Something occurred to me. "Might want to check on all those thralls. The bindings were rush jobs; I'll need to shore them up."

As I stood, Pat followed me. "How long will the, uh, spell last?"

There was a whole lot of arcane arithmetic needed to give that question a precise answer, which I didn't feel like doing. "Hard to say. Few minutes at most. As I said, rush job. But if I shore them up, should get it to an hour. Hopefully Veronica's backup have something more permanent. And can get them some help."

I returned to where the fight had started. One or two of the thralls had apparently slipped their bonds, but there was no sign of them. I hoped they had simply fled. Ryan was among those still tied up. He, and all the others, were lying on the ground in a daze. Pat helped hold each still while I reinforced the magic.

By the time I finished, Veronica had returned in a more relaxed stance. "Vamp slipped outside, along with most of the civvies. You two alright?"

I stood. "Rattled, but ——" I looked at Veronica and saw that she was bleeding. "You've been shot."

Veronica glanced at the wound. "Just a scratch."

I was no medic or biomancer, but I knew gunshot wounds were serious business. "You've been shot!" I rushed up to her. "Hold still." I conjured a tourniquet into existence.

Veronica raised her eyebrows. "You never mentioned you were a wizard."

I tightened the tourniquet. "You never mentioned you were a monster hunter."

Veronica snorted. "Fair enough. Come on, my crew is expecting me."

She led us back out the same entrance we came in through. As we walked, I said, "So … private security firm?"

Veronica laughed. "Technically true. But yeah, we're monster hunters. The Thaleites."

I'd heard of them before. A band of monster hunters unique for their embrace of cutting-edge technologies and scientific methodology as a means of levelling the playing field between human and monster.

Pat seemed to still be processing all the information. "Thaleites?"

Veronica explained, "Named after our founder, Thales. Some Ancient Greek guy. Funnily enough, pretty much every part of the organisation has changed over the last couple of millennia. But we've kept the name."

It was at this point that an unmarked van approached. It stopped in the alley, and a band of fellows in security uniforms exited. Each had a patch on one shoulder, depicting two circles, one inside the other, between lines in a "V". They exchanged a series of code words and military-sounding jargon with Veronica before heading inside. One hung back, taking out some medical supplies and starting to examine Veronica's gunshot wound. Veronica initially pushed them back, saying, "I'm fine."

I snapped, "You've just been shot!"

Veronica shrugged. "I told you, just a scratch."

The medic looked at the wound. "I think the bullet's still in there."

Veronica took a breath to object, but I gave her a pleading look. She groaned. "Ugh, fine. Make it quick."

Veronica sat in the van as the medic worked, Pat and I standing awkwardly outside. Both of us were processing the events of the last few minutes. It was rattling to think just how close I had come to getting killed, or enthralled to a vampire. I didn't envy Pat; his first brush with the supernatural on top of all of that couldn't have been fun. The Thaleites gave us business cards for a front company, Thaltech, which promised it could provide information on the supernatural, as well as take reports for possible hostile supernatural activity.

After a while, Veronica broke the silence. "So, Sarah … do we need to talk?"

I felt like we did, but … "What's there to talk about? It's not like this really changes anything, except maybe that we have more topics of conversation."

"Not all that much more. Not allowed to give too many details about my, you know, *work*. Sensitive information and all that." Despite her words, Veronica seemed to relax. After a moment, she said, "Look, why don't you guys head home? I'll be heading back with my crew. Nothing keeping you here."

Pat's voice was still a little shaky. "Yeah … yeah, we can head home."

Over the next week, I got more than a few phone calls from Pat—questions about the supernatural and about the fight at the club. I answered as best I could; the night had evidently been rough for him, and he needed whatever support he could get. Meanwhile, I found time to go on another date or two with Veronica. It was a relief that I could finally be more open about what I really did for a living, and I could take her to one or two overtly supernatural places.

I also got another invitation to join her at the gym. I'd only grown more smitten with her feats of strength, so I happily accepted. I'd picked up some sportswear in the hopes of this, so I was appropriately dressed when I met her again. I found her in the lobby like last time, but I noticed a couple of bandages around various parts of her body, including around the wound from the nightclub.

I frowned as I approached. "Veronica? You look like you've been through hell."

She shrugged. "Scratches."

I gave her a flat look. "That's what you said after—" I looked around, then leaned in and whispered "—after you were *literally* shot!"

"Went toe-to-toe with a nightmare from the depths. Not as bad as it looks," she whispered back. As I leaned back, she added, "Look, I'm in good enough shape to work out. That's what you're here to watch, right?"

I blushed and assented, figuring that Veronica would have been told enough about her condition by her doctors to make that decision. Soon, she was back to working out. For a while, I enjoyed the show, watching Veronica make a mockery of enough weights to pin most people to the ground a dozen times over. But then, I noticed a worrying red patch appearing on one of her bandages. And it began to spread. "Um … I think you tore a stitch."

Veronica set the weights down, briefly examining the bandage. "Hm." Then, she reached for the weights again.

I winced. "Veronica!"

She looked back up at me. "What?"

"You need to get your stitches put back in!" I sighed. "Look, you're obviously pushing yourself too hard. Let me take you to the hospital, or your doctors. Then you can get your stitches put back in, and then you can relax, and I can fawn over what a big, strong lady you are, with an obviously high pain tolerance."

Veronica looked like she was about to argue, but then she laughed, albeit with a hint of frustration. "Alright."

After handling Veronica's stitches, I persuaded her to come back to my place. There, we lay on my bed, watching a movie on my laptop. After a moment, I thought of another way to show my affection. I slipped behind her and started to gently massage her shoulders. She seemed surprised. "What are you— oh. Oooh, that's the spot." She rolled onto her front to give me better access. I happily moved to massaging her whole body. "Little harder." I obliged, increasing the pressure. "Harder. Hard —actually, just use your whole damn weight." I paused for a moment, worried that that might be too much force, but then again, I wasn't all that heavy, so I stood on her and massaged her with my feet, using my full body weight. Between Veronica's build and her career, the force was warranted. I didn't really know what I was doing, but whatever it was obviously worked, as both of us had soon forgotten about the movie, and Veronica was humming in contentment.

I realised that I might have a possible career as a massage therapist as Veronica dozed off. Then again, considering Veronica's career, and how hard she pushed herself, I could see how she was in dire need of some TLC. I turned off my laptop and tucked her into bed. After brief deliberation, I slid in next to her, slipping underneath her arm.

Chapter Four

At the next roleplaying session, Ryan didn't show. I wasn't terribly surprised; my knowledge of vampires was, until recently, purely academic, but I knew enough to understand Ryan was likely dealing with a lot, not the least of which being coming to terms with the fact that he had tried to attack a friend. I told Abby an altered version of the events at the club, with the gang of vampires replaced with some drug lords and still referring to the Thaleites as Veronica's 'private security firm'.

Before the session started, Pat pulled me aside. "Hey, Sarah, Ryan's … still in bad shape. I was wondering what you knew about churches. Are they, you know, for real?"

I took a deep breath. "That is not an easy question to answer. But, quick summary … there is a pretty powerful being out there, goes by a lot of names, most wizards call it *The One*. It's close to what the Abrahamic religions call *God*. A lot of people say churches, the ones that are aware at least, are pretty good havens for the virtuous. Truth be told, I've heard some pretty mixed reviews about The One and its followers, but as far as I can tell, they at least look out for their own. I know there's a chapel southside, Saint Alban's, that's aware of the supernatural. I think the priest there has actual power."

Pat nodded along. "Okay. How are they against vampires?"

"Pretty good, in theory. A proper priest is effective against a lot of kinds of magic. Never seen it personally, though," I explained, adding, "I'm taking it this is about the club?"

Pat seemed more optimistic now. "I was hoping they could do something for Ryan. He's still struggling with everything that happened, and I think he feels pretty bad for attacking Veronica."

I scoffed. "Like any harm was done."

"She was literally shot!"

"By someone *else*," I pointed out. "Look, I'm not sure how much they can do, but it's worth a shot. Maybe I could take him."

Pat said quietly, "I'd like to go too. Ryan—look, it's a long story, but he was there for me when I needed it."

The chapel was of the Anglican denomination (I pondered what The One thought about the incredibly fractious nature of their so-called worshippers). It was a small brick building without so much as a steeple or a steel crucifix bolted onto the front. Pat, Ryan and I arrived one morning during services.

We entered the building and patiently waited at the back while the priest talked to his congregation about various sins (quite sternly, for the followers of a guy who hung out with prostitutes). After the service drew to a close and the various middle-aged white people milled about over refreshments, I approached the priest—someone who'd only need a quick haircut for an impressive Friar Tuck cosplay. "Er, hi. My friends and I have recently had an encounter with …" I pulled from my shirt an amulet marking me as a low-ranking member of the Circle of Magi "dark forces. We were hoping for some advice. In private, if you don't mind."

The priest examined the amulet (a sapphire, emerald and ruby at three points around a circle) and nodded. "I see. Come, my child." He led the three of us into a back room with some decades-old couches surrounding a coffee table. He sat, gesturing for us to do the same. "Now, what appears to be the issue?"

As I sat, I explained, "Ryan here had a run-in with some vampires and got enthralled. A … friend of mine managed to kill the vampire, but Ryan's still in a bad way. I was wondering if you knew any way of speeding his recovery."

The priest's expression fell, and he stared at the floor, silent. There was a long pause. Pat broke the silence. "Is something wrong?"

As he searched for what to say, a man entered from the back, a burly fellow in a trench coat and covered in Christian iconography tattoos (which, I had to admit, looked pretty sick). "Father, you heard our orders."

The priest gave the man a pleading look. "He's after help! Did Jesus not die so that he could be absolved of his sins!?"

Something was very wrong here. I slipped my hand into my handbag and started gathering mana, just in case. The man in the coat, meanwhile, said, "That's not for you or me to decide."

Pat stood. "If there's a problem, maybe we should leave."

The man pulled a gun. "You need to ——"

I withdrew my hand, casting a spell, the same wind blast I used at the club. Our attacker was clearly caught off guard and hit the wall with what had to be a painful impact. I bolted, Pat and Ryan right behind me. We pushed through the confused church congregation outside and raced to the car. Too panicked to bother with seatbelts, we slid into the seats, casting panicked glances over our shoulders. Pat fumbled briefly with the ignition before starting the car.

A gunshot. A shattered window. A bloody wound in Ryan's shoulder.

Pat was already slamming the accelerator, and we managed to pull into the street and away before any more shots landed on us. But we weren't safe yet. I called to Pat, "Ryan's been hit! We need to get him to hospital!"

Pat didn't need any more coaxing. He probably broke at least a dozen road laws, careening to the hospital, but I hoped any police would be understanding after seeing the gunshot wound. Meanwhile, I rang Veronica.

Ring… (Come on, come on…)

Ring… (Was there someone following us?)

Ring… (Ryan's losing blood.)

Click "Veronica Wainwright."

"Ryan was shot! At the church, there was a man in a trench coat, said something about orders ——"

Veronica's tone quickly turned from disinterested to serious. "Alright, calm down. First, are you being shot at right now?"

I peered out through the car's windows. "Uh, no. We're driving him to hospital now. Light traffic, thankfully."

"Alright, then tell me everything. That way we can decide if more needs to happen."

I did so. Veronica replied, "Weird, I knew the Anglicans had shooters, but they never … look, I'll report this to my crew. They'll know what to do. The hospital should be safe enough; public, with a lot of cameras. Not too many hits go on there."

"Sure, sure. Alright. Talk to you soon."

"Bye." *Click.*

The ride to the hospital was tense, with Ryan losing a worrying amount of blood, but we eventually arrived. We piled out of the car. When Ryan stumbled, Pat outright carried him to the emergency room. As soon as the doors opened, he called out, "He's been shot!" This was enough to get the attention of the medical staff, and soon Ryan was being wheeled further inside the hospital on a gurney.

Adrenaline finally wearing off, Pat asked, "So, what happened back there?"

I whispered back, "Your guess is as good as mine. I've heard church agents can be overzealous, but that …"

There was a long silence. Finally, Pat whispered back, "What do we do now?"

I thought about that for a while. The church knew our faces, and they had Pat's number plate. It would also be likely that they had sympathetic officials that could get them Pat's address from that.

Eventually, I thought of a workable plan. "You can stay at my place tonight. They probably won't know about it, and I can set up some defences. Block the door, bar the windows. Keep us secure until we hear back from V. Ryan should be safe enough here."

Then, I had a further idea. I called Veronica again. "Veronica? Pat and I are worried they will come for us. They probably saw Pat's plate, so I have told him to stay at my place until we hear back from your people. But I was thinking, could you stay as well? It'll be a bit cramped, but after the club …"

Despite the serious situation, I could hear a smile in Veronica's voice. "Sure. Don't worry, it'll take a lot to get through me."

After Pat arranged repairs for his car windows, we took a taxi to within walking distance of my place. We agreed to say that if the police asked, we'd give a mostly accurate account, again replacing Ryan's brush with vampirism with a brush with hard drugs, and my spellcasting with a blast of pepper spray.

As soon as I got home, I pulled out my spell book and started planning some magical fortifications. There wasn't much I could do to outright stop a determined and well-equipped attacker, but I could at least make it so anyone doing so would require something very big and loud, and slow them enough for Veronica to wake up and dispatch whatever threat arose.

For the door, I started with the mundane block-it-with-a-chair approach. I jammed the mechanisms that allowed the windows to open, then started painting runes on the inside that improved the structural integrity of the glass. I also assembled some runic circles that would slow anything moving too fast as a defence against projectiles.

Veronica arrived late in the afternoon, wearing a ballistic vest and carrying a sports bag that I suspected held weapons. Letting her inside took some time, as it involved dismantling all the defences I'd already set up. As I let her in, I started explaining what I'd set up. She nodded approvingly. "Nice work. Honestly, I hope they come. Don't want all this preparation to go to waste."

I laughed nervously. "I mean, if I didn't do the preparation and they did attack, then I'd be dead. But I think I've been shot at enough for one week. Or month. Or life."

Veronica chuckled, opening the bag to reveal, as I suspected, a few guns and some ammunition. I pulled out a set of blankets and made a makeshift sleeping spot on the ground for Pat. Veronica slept on the bed, and I slept on Veronica. For all the dangers of the day, Veronica was a calming presence. I'd given all my blankets to Pat, but Veronica was more than warm enough. She wrapped an arm around me, and the feeling of her built muscles reminded me that anyone trying to get through her would have a *very* long day.

The night passed without incident, save for Pat getting a text from Ryan; he was going to be alright. We made plans to visit him before lunch. The hour arrived soon enough, and I headed to the hospital. Pat was already there, calmly talking with Ryan. The conversation was slow and awkward; Ryan was still recovering from the effects of enthrallment, and the gunshot wound (and resulting regime of drugs) on top of that had left him in poor condition.

As we talked, I received a text from Veronica. *One of my crew wants an account.* Not long after, a man in a simple navy suit and tie with a practised smile and short beard entered. "Ryan O'Mannister? I'm John Larrick, Thaltech security. I was hoping you'd answer a few questions about the shooting."

Ryan and I told him everything, even the supernatural events (after I peered out of the door to make sure no-one was listening). Just as we were wrapping up the story, Pat called, "Shit!"

We all glanced in his direction, where he was gazing out of the window. Something had drawn his attention. He turned back to us. "It's him!"

I hurried to the window, where I saw a pair of large vans in the parking lot. A band of men in trench coats, at least 20, was walking towards the hospital. I also saw the man that had shot Ryan. My heart raced. I spun around and faced the Thaleite agent. "It's them, the people that attacked us. Must be tying up loose ends."

John rushed towards the window, pressing a finger to an earpiece. I half-heard him whispering a stream of military codes and jargon, before he listened to some reply. He turned back to us. "We have agents en route, but it will take them a few minutes to get here."

Ryan sat up, visibly panicked. "What about security?"

The agent started to leave the room. "I'll alert them, but they can't fight off a determined attack."

I called after the agent, "Get back here quick, I'll barricade the room!"

The conversation was replaced by the terrifyingly ordinary sounds of a hospital. I started scanning the room for entrances, and things I could use as makeshift fortifications. Despite the room's small size, there were three doors. Luckily, the room was also littered with shelves and trolleys full of various medical sundries. I hoped they weren't too expensive as I wheeled them into position to jam the doors. When John returned, I blocked the door he came in through, then started inscribing runes on the door and conjuring barriers.

Then the gunfire started. I tried to tune it out and focus on my spellcasting, but it was so damn *loud!* I had to redraw the same rune four times, my hands shaking. Despite that, it was only a matter of time before I'd done all I could. The doors were heavily barred and blocked, but it would only take someone with a big axe and some patience to get through.

The gunfire died down. An achingly slow minute passed, and I heard a dozen boots hitting the ground outside the hospital. I heard the door outside rattle, followed by conversation. Someone wedged a crowbar in the gap between the door and the frame. I closed my eyes and channelled my will into the runes, granting them strength. But it was a stop-gap measure, and the crowbar was soon joined by another.

John spoke into his earpiece, "They're right outside, and the wizard's spells aren't going to hold forever. Give me an ETA!" A pause, then he spoke to me. "My people are 60 seconds out. Just hold them!"

Sixty seconds was a damn long time to pay attention. But I had to try. After all, my life depended on it. I focused, drawing upon my animal will to survive. It bought us a few more precious seconds. But eventually, the door buckled and finally came off its hinges. The attackers moved to push away the shelf I'd shoved between us and them, but Pat and the Thaleite rushed to keep it in position. As they strained against the attackers, I improvised some more runes, shoring up the barrier, buying yet a little more time.

Gunfire resumed in a lower level of the hospital. I heard some chatter from our attackers, and they stopped pressing against the barricade, apparently turning to fight a new threat. I looked at the Thaleite. "Is that them?"

He sighed in relief. "Hopefully. And the enemy are more concerned about the people shooting at them than us."

I slumped against the wall, panting in exhaustion. "At least they're smart."

Pat briefly peered above the barricade before ducking back down. "Think Veronica's with them? The Thaleites, I mean?"

I shrugged. "We'll see."

There was a tense few minutes as sporadic gunfire worked its way through the hospital. Eventually, the deafening sounds could be heard just outside. Then, silence. As the ringing in my ears faded, I recognised Veronica's voice. I heard her trade a few code words with John, but I was already dismantling the barricade.

When I saw her, I would have struggled to recognise her if not for her voice. She was dressed head to toe in heavy armour painted a splotchy dark grey, her face obscured by goggles and a respirator. She was carrying a massive rifle with a dozen technical-looking attachments. When she saw me, she pulled off her respirator, letting me see her face. "Sarah! You alright?"

I flung myself at her, wrapping my arms around her. "Oh, thank all the gods! Fuck, they nearly killed me!"

Veronica gently patted me on the back. "Hey, hey. I'm here."

John politely coughed. "Ahem. Forgive my interruption, but you should ——"

He was interrupted by a bright glow from up the corridor. I peered out and saw strands of light form and shift, a man kitted out like Veronica levelling a shotgun towards the phenomenon. Space fragmented and reformed, as if reality was rearranging itself to accommodate something new. The lights shifted, reformed, and materialised in the form of three men in suits and dark sunglasses.

My heart sank. "Angels."

John adjusted his suit and strode out into the hall. "Parley?"

The angels reached into their suits and pulled pistols. Veronica pushed me back into cover as her comrade moved in front of John, and the gunfire started. Any ordinary humans would have been cut down in a second, but the only ordinary humans here were ducking for cover. Whatever armour Veronica and her comrade were wearing must have been effective, as the impacts of bullets staggered them, but they kept shooting. The angels, unconstrained by the limits of a mortal body, dodged the bullets flying at them, somersaulting into cover.

I alternated between being impelled by my curiosity to stick my head out and my self-preservation instincts to duck my head back down. Veronica was moving from cover to cover, trying to catch the angels as they moved with inhuman speed. Gritting her teeth in frustration, she slung her rifle around her back, pulling out a pistol and knife in its place (though the knife was so massive it might have been more accurate to call it a short sword). She charged towards the angels, pistol firing and knife ready. The angels met her in hand-to-hand combat.

The angels were stronger and faster than any human could hope to be. They weren't human at all: divine machines in mortal guise. Their minds were as sharp as their bodies, quick processing speed coupled with a level of foresight granted by their divinity. The ways of combat were encoded into their very being.

Veronica was a match for two of them.

The fighting was blindingly fast, limbs turning into blurs of motion, punches and parries interspersed with gunshots as Veronica and the angels battled. It looked wild and chaotic, but beneath it there was an undercurrent of strategy, like a lightning-fast match between chess masters, each side trying to outmanoeuvre the other, limbs and weapons moving in tactic and counter-tactic. Debris rained as missed shots put holes in plaster and medical equipment.

Veronica's comrade wasn't doing as well, fighting an angel himself. He wasn't out of the fight yet, but the angel had landed several shots, and I knew even the best ballistic vest couldn't completely absorb a bullet's impact. I grimaced; this fight could go either way.

I started analysing the situation strategically. The Thaleite soldiers were better armoured and had heavier weapons, but the angels were much faster. If I could find a way to mitigate their speed, the Thaleites would have the advantage. I mentally flicked through the spells I knew and thought of one that could do the job: a simple conjuration spell that would summon a sticky slime.

Keeping my head low, I started drawing the requisite runes on the ground.

My danger ring thrummed, and I filled my protective wards with mana in time to turn a lethal shot into something that just sent me sprawling. I heard Veronica roar in rage, tackling the angel that had fired on me. But the bold move left her open; the other angel fired a shot, and I saw blood spray from the rear of her knee, where there was a gap between armour plates.

Veronica kept fighting, wrestling with one angel while firing at the other with her pistol. Seeing Veronica in such danger pushed me past my fear, and I resumed casting the spell. Veronica was holding the angel's attention, and I managed to finish forming the runes. I pulled the mana through the runes, gave it form with my incantations. Soon a grey, sticky slime was oozing out from the runic circle and steadily flowing to where the fights were taking place.

The angels must have figured out my plan, or else simply assumed the goo was bad news for them, as they started backing off. But the fight turned in the Thaleite's favour: gunfire could be heard from up the hall, making that route just as dangerous, if not more so. The fight moved back towards me, but that was good. The goo worked, and the angels slowed.

The angel Veronica had grappled slipped free in an elaborate manoeuvre that involved twisting Veronica's arm in a way that definitely broke something, but it rolled back to the goo. Veronica pressed the attack, rushing forward and landing a solid headbutt. With impressive instincts, Veronica broke off the attack to evade another pair of bullets from the second advancing angel. With her good arm, Veronica turned and shot the first angel as it stood. The goo slowed its holy speed enough for the bullets to land solidly in its leg, and as it stumbled, Veronica landed a masterful kick that broke its neck.

The second angel propelled itself in a jump from the wall, avoiding the goo long enough to land a fast and painful strike on Veronica's jaw. The two landed in a heap, the ooze slowing what could have been a deft roll. The pair stood and resumed hand-to-hand, Veronica fighting with one arm.

Those firing from up the hall advanced, revealing themselves to be more Thaleite soldiers. Veronica noticed her allies and pushed everything she had into kicking the angel back. The pair disengaged, and the other Thaleites took the chance to unload a hail of lead at the angel. A few scored hits, leaving the angel too weak to dodge the rest of the incoming bullets. Up the hall, three soldiers had ganged up on the third angel, finally bringing it down after a struggle. The dead angels warped, shifting into dozens of interlocking runic rings, before dissipating into a stream of light. The fight was finally over.

With a small effort of will, I dismantled the magic keeping the ooze in existence, like pulling a loose thread, and it vanished without trace. Veronica was leaning on the wall, teeth gritted in pain. There were a dozen dents in her armour where bullets had impacted, and her arm hung limp. Despite her obviously severe injuries, she was still trying to stand. One of the Thaleite soldiers rushed up to her and slung her good arm around his shoulder. She muttered, "I'm good, I'm good …"

To which the soldier responded, "The fuck you're good. Fuck, we're in a hospital, how hard can it be to get you medical attention?"

John stood and straightened, adjusting his tie, and turned to where Pat, Ryan and I were cowering. "Ahem. We need to clear the area before the police arrive; if they ask, simply say that some unidentified attackers were dispatched by unidentified soldiers. Don't need to go all that far from the truth."

Ryan asked "Are … are they going to come back?"

"The church fellows? I don't think so. A small group like that could only have so many combat-ready agents. Honestly, I wasn't expecting this many. Try not to worry about it. My people will sort it out." As he left with the rest of the Thaleites, he added, "Oh, and thanks for the help. That trick with the, uh, goo was actually quite impressive."

Soon, the 'gang war' in the middle of the hospital was all over the news. Luckily, the police swallowed our story, and the news crews were more interested in the civilians that were in the lobby and the killed security guards, so we got through the next couple of days without too many cameras pointed at us.

Once things settled down a bit, I called Veronica. "Hey, Veronica? It's me …"

"Hey, sweetie. How are you?"

"Rattled, but no sign of those … you know."

"That's good."

"Look, you're asking how I am, but last I saw of you …"

"Yeah, yeah. Look, I'm fine. I'm tough, and the doctors here are great ——"

I heard a voice call at Veronica, "Then listen to our damn advice!"

Veronica snapped back at the voice, "It's not that bad!"

The voice replied, "Yes, it is!"

Veronica huffed in frustration before returning her attention to me. "Anyway, I'll be fine."

I paused. I had a lot I wanted to say, and I had to decide what to say first. "I've been meaning to ask … how did you do that? Fight the angels, I mean."

"I mean, you were there, weren't you?"

"Yeah, but I mean, those things are superhuman, and you fought *two at once!* Honestly, I wasn't sure you needed my help. How the hell did you pull that off?"

"I, uh … I'm not sure how much I can say about that. I'll just say that running with this crew has some, uh, *perks.*"

Not much of an answer, and I was still sure something big had to be going on. But there wasn't any way I could get more out of her, not over the phone. "Where are you?"

"Thaleite medical facility. Can't say more than that."

"No chance of me visiting then."

"Nah. But you can call."

"That'll do, then. And Veronica? Take care of yourself."

"Oh, come on, you too?"

"I care about you, Veronica! A lot."

"…"

"…"

"…"

I finally broke the silence. "Look, I'll let you get your rest. But I'll call again in a couple of days, okay?"

"Sure, looking forward to it."

Considering Veronica had literally saved my life, for a second time now, I was as eager as ever to do something for her. I couldn't do anything in person, of course, but I guessed correctly that the Thaleite's front companies would be happy to deliver a package. So, I sent her a bouquet of flowers and some mixed-berry ice cream I noticed she liked.

The next afternoon, I gave her that phonecall I promised. She answered pretty quickly.

"Hey, honey! Did you get the package I sent you?" I asked.

Veronica sounded … *embarrassed?* "Oh, uh, yeah. It was …" As she trailed off, I could hear some distant jeers from someone else in the room. Veronica proceeded to turn away from the microphone, and while I couldn't hear exactly what was said, I was certain it was a threat. How sincere it was was something I'd never figure out. A second later, Veronica returned to the phone. She whispered, "It was nice. Thanks."

I paced around my room awkwardly. "Has your squad been giving you a hard time?"

A pause. "Yeah." Back in a whisper that I had to turn up my phone's volume to hear, she added, "A bouquet of flowers and tub of ice cream isn't really 'spec ops'."

I shifted my grip on my phone, worried that I'd done something wrong. "Do you want me to stop?"

"… No."

I overheard Veronica and her squad mates share some none-too-kind words. I made sure to make it up by flattering her a little before I needed to hang up.

Chapter Five

A few days later, I was contacted again by the Thaleites. The church group that had attacked us had been handled, and all of its members aware of the supernatural 'neutralised' (I decided not to ask what that meant). Apparently, they'd received orders from angels that everyone touched by dark forces, including both current and former vampiric thralls, were to be killed. Luckily, there wasn't much communication between churches, particularly of different denominations, so they had probably lost track of Ryan, but they advised us all to avoid churches until further notice.

Ryan started looking better over the next few weeks. He was still very much rattled by his repeated near-death experiences, but the effects of the vampire's enthralment began to wear off, and over time he recovered from the gunshot wound (expressing outright disbelief when I mentioned Veronica seemed to think she could just walk such injuries off).

Veronica and I spoke over the phone frequently, and after a couple of weeks, she was released from medical care, though with advice to take it easy, which she pointedly ignored. She quickly decided to make up for lost time, taking me out to dinner before dropping me home. Her over-enthusiasm that night resulted in her accidentally dislocating my jaw.

It was one hundred per cent worth it.

I kept showing my support for the Green Hands, hoping that building their support would eventually have an impact on the rising demon problem. After a lengthy meeting, the party members were approached by a small band of pixies, which handed out a series of letters containing invitations to a ball hosted by one of the innumerable warring faerie courts. I'd heard faerie balls were invariably havens of political manoeuvring and elaborate social games, but I'd never actually attended one. The faeries promised a wealth of entertainments (as well as a strict no-murder policy), and I heard the other Hands discussing the potential benefits of making an appearance. And each invitation allowed the bearer to bring an additional guest …

"Hey, V. Want to attend a faerie ball? With me?"

Veronica sounded mildly surprised. "Never pegged you as the faerie ball type."

Setting aside the innumerable lewd jokes I could have made from her choice of words, I said, "Part of it's political. My party's thinking about making a few deals. But I've never been to one before, and I kind of want to see what they're like."

"Which court? I'm kind of on the shit list of more than one. Risks of the job." She sounded awfully casual about the matter. Then again, knowing her, any fey seeking vengeance would have to deal with a hail of iron-jacketed bullets.

"Uh …" I glanced again at the invitation. "Court of Vines."

"Okay, they're pretty good. Sure." She then added, "Oh, I'm guessing no bringing iron?"

"Yeah, it's a pretty big insult." To the fey, carrying iron was like carrying a biohazard.

The day came, and this time I had time to make sure I was properly dressed for the occasion. After extensive deliberation, I settled on a sea-blue dress with wavy patterns woven on it in sequins. I met Veronica in a local arboretum, one containing a gateway to the fey realms. She was wearing an imposing dark grey three-piece suit and tie, with subtle pinstripes that complemented her already amazonian height, and a white undershirt. The suit was likely custom-tailored; it fit her perfectly, despite her size.

She gave me that confident, but not arrogant, smile. "Hey, puppy."

I was stunned. "You look … um …" I gulped. Veronica's appearance occupied so much of my mind that I didn't have enough left to find a compliment.

Veronica snickered; my stunned response seemed to be compliment enough. "Come on. We have dancing to do."

A spell on the invitation opened a portal between two trees, and we found ourselves in a wild, warped city, with plants of every shape and size interweaved with buildings just as varied.

Outside our destination, a pair of burly hobgoblins crammed into security guard uniforms checked the invitations of those attending the party. I showed them mine, and they let Veronica and I enter. The interior of the building was like a conference hall in an art galley formed by someone still getting the hang of Euclidean space. Amidst several well-stocked banquet tables were dozens of folk, mundane and supernatural. Wizards danced with werecreatures, elves dined with monster hunters, and priests talked politics with vampires.

I found a few other Green Hands settled towards the end of one banquet table. I was supposed to be mingling and making friends, but a quick check confirmed that the other Hands had that handled. So, I invited Veronica to dance. Neither of us had the faintest clue what we were doing, bar holding our hands in a particular position and slowly spinning around, but we didn't let that ruin our night. What *did* throw something of a wrench into the works was us realising we were surrounded by a squad of burly-looking men in suits with none-too-pleased expressions on their faces.

We stopped dancing. I pushed my body up closer to Veronica for protection, or at least the sense thereof. Veronica wrapped an arm around me and addressed the men. "Can I help you?"

A woman approached, an older one wearing a long golden dress that walked the thin line between 'standing out' and 'gaudy'. "You're a bold woman to show your face here."

Veronica cocked her head. "Do I know you?"

The woman's eyes darkened. "You killed my son."

"Gonna have to narrow it down."

The woman snarled. "Did his life mean so little to you?"

"I mean, I kill a *lot* of people. Kind of the day job." Veronica's tone was remarkably casual, but I could see her glancing quickly between the woman and her guards, mentally planning for the fight.

"A simple business transaction in Melbourne. That's what it was supposed to be, anyway." The woman said with cold hatred.

This did seem to remind Veronica of something. "Ooooh, you're part of the Family!"

I blinked. "What?"

Veronica muttered, "Supernatural organised crime. My people and theirs have our … disagreements."

I decided further questions could wait until there wasn't a serious risk of being shot. "Um, we are guests of a fey, and I read in the invitation that there was a no violence clause. So … look, maybe we could talk this out later?"

The other party guests were starting to notice the scene, taking a few steps away from the potential fight. We were approached by a fey lady; something not quite human, like a supermodel when the editor is a bit too generous with the airbrush. "Heeeey, now, do we have a little drama?"

The Family woman didn't take her eyes off Veronica. "This woman killed my son. Honoured host, if you would be so kind as to … eject her, I would be grateful. And consider it a small favour to be paid in kind."

The host grinned. "Certainly. You two are hereby uninvited."

Before I could suggest leaving, the Family woman pulled a gun from her handbag. Perhaps she expected the goons surrounding us to dissuade any attempts at fighting. Regardless, she obviously didn't expect Veronica's speed. The moment the woman extended her arm to shoot, Veronica rushed forward and grabbed it, twirling her between herself and the goons. In the same fluid motion, she shoved me to the floor. I was too busy ducking for cover to see exactly what happened next, but there were a few gunshots, some punches, a few more gunshots, and guests screaming and scrambling for cover.

I poked my head back up to see what was going on. The Family woman and her goons were all dead, and the fey lady was taking a few cautious steps back as what looked like another wave approached. Veronica, now armed with one of the goon's pistols, took my hand and led me towards the banquet tables, where a few bystanders were cowering. With her other hand, she engaged the remaining goons, keeping herself between me and the attackers.

I saw her stumble as something—something far too likely to be a bullet—impacted her hard in the back. She rolled with the hit, using its momentum to push the two of us over a table before kicking it over to use as cover. As she shifted position, bullet holes appearing where she just was, I saw a pair of holes in the back of her suit. But, strangely, there was a distinct lack of blood, and while Veronica was visibly in pain, she was very much in fighting condition. The suit must have been lined with bullet-resistant material.

The fey lady snarled, revealing teeth too straight and white to be human. She raised a hand, and vines burst from the ground, entangling Veronica. She gritted her teeth and burst out, turning her gun on the lady without breaking a sweat. She staggered back, flesh turning to bark as the bullets impacted. She retreated deeper into her hall as her security hobgoblins rushed to join the fight.

I grimaced. Fighting a fey lady in her hall was no small feat. Probably about the same difficulty as fighting two angels at once. Which meant Veronica could certainly use help. Fortunately, unlike angels, fey had a very clear weakness. The trick would be exploiting it; there was no way any fey would allow someone to bring iron to an event, and the same magical inertia that made iron so effective against fey made it extremely difficult to conjure; it was certainly beyond my abilities if it was possible at all.

Fortunately, there were much more experienced wizards in attendance. As Veronica slotted some more mooks, I crawled over to where another of the Green Hands was cowering, coming across an older wizard with sagging jowls named Ruth. She gave me a furious glare as I approached. I called over the sound of gunfire, "I had no idea this would happen! Look, we need iron. Ideas?"

"I'm a transmutation specialist; that's conjuration! Unless you've already got iron." Her tone made it clear she didn't believe I could.

I thought for a moment. "The human body contains iron."

She blinked. "Are you going to donate?"

I pointed to one of the Family goons whose brain matter was decorating the floor. "He's not using it."

Ruth looked conflicted, but after I gave her a pleading look, she slunk out of cover to where the dead bodies lay. Luckily, she was still a guest at the party, so the hobgoblins couldn't shoot her (not that Veronica wasn't a far greater threat anyway). She drew some runes on the ground, and an ethereal glow appeared in her hands as she spoke an incantation.

Meanwhile, Veronica had dispatched the second wave of hapless goons and was taking from them fresh magazines. Seeing no more immediate threats, I called, "Honey, do you want to, you know, get of out here?"

Veronica checked her gun's chamber. "This bitch ruined our night so she could curry favour with the Family. She's paying for that."

I shifted nervously. "Well … I'll catch up when Ruth's finished making you something iron."

Veronica nodded. "Thanks. I owe you one."

Ruth grumbled, "Damn right you do."

Veronica followed the fey lady up a hall, careful to check her corners. As she peered around one, she ducked back just in time to avoid a few bullets. She returned fire before advancing beyond my sight. While I couldn't see the fight, the gunshots echoed, leaving me to pace uncomfortably while Ruth worked.

A minute later, she'd assembled what amounted to an iron nail. She handed it to me. "This is the best I can make you."

I shrugged—iron was iron, and Veronica had proved her skill with far less. "It'll do. Thanks."

Following Veronica through the spatially warped maze of a fey lady's domain would have, under normal circumstances, proved to be a very difficult task, full of false turns, shifting passageways and awkward gravitational arrangements, but Veronica had conveniently left a trail of blood for me to follow. I caught up to her as she was engaged in hand-to-hand with an athletic man wearing a leather jacket over a ballistic vest. He seemed to be holding up to Veronica's superhuman strength and speed; I guessed he was a human that had been granted fey power in exchange for guard duty. The tricky thing was that the fey lady was just up the hall, and while the risk of friendly fire prevented her from using her higher power spells, a few vines were slowing Veronica down.

Appraising the room's unusual geometry, I noticed the walkway extended up the wall to the roof above. Approaching it, I found that gravity nearby focused on the walkway, allowing me to get up to the roof above Veronica with no more trouble than a little disorientation and nausea. I called out to her before dropping the nail down to her. She caught it with her teeth before resuming her lightning-fast fistfight.

When the other human next lunged, Veronica twisted to fling him off a walkway and send him spiralling through the maze of spacetime that constituted the fey lair. She then spat the iron nail into her hand, used it to tear apart the vines restraining her, and rushed the fey lady. With a shriek of terror, she sent a barrage of thorns at Veronica, who simply raised her suit's lapel in front of her head, the thorns shredding the suit's outer layer but unable to penetrate its lining. She crashed into the fey lady, and both tumbled to the ground. As the lady's bodyguard rushed to aid, Veronica took the nail and drove it through her skull.

The bodyguard slowed as the lady shrieked and died, the entire domain rumbling with the loss of its liege. I saw the eerie glow fade from his eyes as he said "Well, there goes my job. I'm unemployed now. Hope you're happy."

Veronica stood, wiping some blood of uncertain origin from her cheek. "Considering you literally just tried to kill me, I'm pretty content."

The two warriors stared at each other for a while, panting heavily, each wondering if the other would go for the kill. I walked back to normal ground. "Hey, maybe we should leave before any of her friends show up."

As we walked away, the bodyguard not pursuing, Veronica examined her suit. "Ugh, the tailors are going to be pissed."

I smiled demurely. "I dunno. I think a little battle damage looks good." As Veronica giggled, I added, "Why don't we go back to my place? We can watch a movie and you can get some rest. After we get you checked out."

Veronica rolled her eyes. "Relax, puppy, this thing's bulletproof."

I gave her a flat look. "V, you were hit by bullets. All that kinetic energy had to go somewhere, and I'm pretty sure that somewhere involves your bones. Can we just make sure nothing's shattered?"

Veronica sighed. "Alright. But if I'm staying in hospital, you're staying with me."

"Deal."

At the end of that week's roleplaying session, Veronica pulled me aside. "Hey, I've been thinking about the party, and the hospital … I want to teach you how to fight."

"What? *Me?*" I was a quarter of her mass, at most. I bruised easily, and every time there was trouble, I couldn't do much more than cower.

Not that this was news to Veronica. "Yeah. I … tend to get into fights. Happened my whole life—kind of why I made a career out of it. Anyway, if you're with me all the time, I'd feel better knowing that you at least knew enough to not get instantly killed by a lucky grunt." She had a point; I knew that I had been in real danger more than once while at her side. And for all her brawn and skill, she was only one woman.

So, a few days later, I picked out some sportswear for myself, and Veronica took me to the local gym's boxing ring. After giving me the 'appraising' kind of look I'd only take from her, she handed me some gloves and started walking me through the correct technique to form a punch. Her teaching was very hands-on—perhaps more than it needed to be—but we were both enjoying ourselves.

Once I got the hang of throwing a proper punch, Veronica moved on to teaching me how to block a punch. She started very slowly, focusing on making sure I had the technique down. Once she was satisfied with that, she said, "Alright, let's see if you can do this when I'm going a bit faster."

I nodded, settling into the stance Veronica had taught me; I was nervous, but not unpleasantly so. "Alright, hit me."

WHAM!

I came to on Veronica's lap, an icepack on my aching jaw. She was gently stroking my hair with a deeply worried expression on her face. I blinked, trying to clear my head. "Ngh … wha?"

"Puppy, I am so damn sorry. I don't know what I was thinking; there was no way you could have handled that." She was speaking fast, trying to push out all her repentance as fast as she could. "Stupid of me. I must have slipped into sparring mode. Me and my crew beat the crap out of each other all the time. But you're not one of us. And I forget how strong I am, sometimes. I really should have gone slower."

Meanwhile, I ran my tongue across my teeth, relieved to find they were all present and accounted for. Satisfied there was no permanent damage, I hushed Veronica with a finger to her lips. "Buy me an ice cream and we're even."

Veronica sighed audibly in relief. "Deal."

We called it a day, but we talked, and I was happy to resume training. We started again the following week, when she moved on to teaching me some basic grapples. She was happy to demonstrate each move on me, and I certainly didn't mind her pinning me to the mat, not that she needed any special technique to completely immobilise me. She was impressively gentle, despite what she was training me for. She knew I wasn't a tenth as tough as her, and she managed to keep her immense strength in check (while a tiny part of my brain wished that she didn't, my rationality and fear managed to keep that part in check). I also managed to successfully execute the pins on her, though I was certain she could have just forced her way out of them.

As I managed to get her into another pin, I whispered to her, "Next time, we're not doing this in public."

Veronica's grin showed that she knew *exactly* what I meant.

Months passed slowly. In addition to Veronica's training, I'd taken to reinforcing my flat with some longer-term supernatural defences. It took a lot of time and effort, but I'd more than had my fill of action, and I didn't want to run into any more zealots, faeries or hired guns. Fortunately, the Thaleites seemed to have been right, as I wasn't confronted again. But I noticed more preachers and doomsayers on the streets, and every other day I heard word on the supernatural grapevine that the demons were getting yet bolder.

Veronica was a light in all that darkness. I felt safe around her, and she promised that if anything happened to me, she'd visit a bloody vengeance on the perpetrator. She was still prone to leaving for days, or even weeks, at a time on short notice, on some mission or other for the Thaleites, but I didn't mind, instead preferring to think about all she was doing to hold back the tide. And when she came back from a long mission, when she saw me next, her face would light up like she was coming home.

Over time, it started to sink in that Veronica loved me. It wasn't easy to get my head around; what the hell did she even see in me? I was just a tiny nerd with a little magic. But she saw something, apparently, and she was always happy to talk to or spend time with me. Doubly so when spending time involved physical contact of some kind—holding hands, kissing, cuddling (not to mention sparring). I certainly didn't mind the attention; I enjoyed the physical contact too, especially because being held by someone so big and strong made me feel safe.

One night, Veronica came to my place for another night of cuddling (and more). I opened the door and greeted her with a smile.

Hers was just as wide. "What's been going on?"

"I made something for you." I was brimming with enthusiasm. I led her further into my apartment and opened a drawer, pulling a rune-covered cylinder with a switch and slot for a battery. I flipped the switch and a circular translucent barrier formed in front of the cylinder. I held it in front of me. "It's a shield projector! The shield's not all that tough, but it should regenerate quickly."

I flicked the switch off and handed it to Veronica. She activated it herself, examining how much of her it covered (just shy of her whole torso) and moving it to various positions, miming aiming a pistol around it. She smiled. "This is neat! Thanks, honey. I'm sure it'll come in handy." She flicked it off and slid it into her pocket.

I added, "It's battery powered, but it uses off-the-shelf batteries. I had an electrician friend of mine do all the wiring."

Veronica blinked. "Battery powered?"

"Well, you're not a wizard, so you can't draw on your own internal mana, but wizards have been drawing power from lightning for centuries. It wasn't too hard to modify those runes to work for any source of electrical power, and my friend says the circuit is a really simple one."

Veronica laughed. "Battery-powered magic. Genius. Next time I'm at the firing range, I'll check how much punishment this thing can handle."

I rubbed the back of my neck. "I'm not entirely sure. Honestly, not sure if it would even stop a bullet."

Veronica gently picked me up (I *loved* it when she did that). "Honey, you just made something for me. How long did that take you?"

I stammered, "I mean, I had a friend ——"

"Not the point. You *made* this *for me*. That means a lot." She got a predatory glint in her eye. "Now, why don't I show you how grateful I am?"

My research cabal wasn't directly sabotaged by demons, but it suffered more than one delay due to destruction of supplies or injuries to staff, which meant a few nights of overtime to catch up. After an hour of work, during which my attention span dwindled to near nothing, we created a rune which did nothing but fizzle out.

Our research lead, a short man with a long beard named Paul, grunted in frustration. "Well, that was bust. Alright people, get those results down, then we're done for the night." That gave me a last kick of energy, enough to write down everything I needed to in time to follow some of my co-workers out of the door. We entered the larger Prismatic Spire, a labyrinthine web of walkways and offices on the interior of a vast cylinder, where gravity pulled towards the cylinder's exterior and a shaft of bright light ran through the middle in lieu of a sun. Navigating the place was something that took practice, and I tried to stick to well-beaten paths.

As my colleagues and I walked together towards the portal back to Earth, one of them turned towards a dark corner, visibly alarmed. "Does anyone else sense something?"

Attuning my senses to the currents of mana that underpinned reality, I realised I could indeed sense something dark and twisted approaching. I could tell my colleagues felt the same. One of them, Will, called out for the sentinels, the Spire's law enforcement. Meanwhile, the dark forces started to take a physical form: a horrid blood-red ooze that was seeping out from shadowy corners and gathering in a festering pile.

The whole lot of us turned and ran, only to find yet more of the dark matter pooling across the street. The ooze began to solidify into bone and sinew, then it shaped itself into a squat parody of a human with elongated limbs.

A demon.

More demons started emerging from all around us, and the sentinels were nowhere to be seen. Another of my colleagues, Harriet, a lanky woman with an overabundance of hair, called out, "Get through the portal!" We rushed down the street, quickly finding the circle of runes and carefully tunnelled hole that would lead us back to Earth. We rushed through, thankful that these demons weren't the fastest.

We regrouped on the other side of the portal. Unfortunately, it was early nightfall in the city, and the streets here were mostly empty. I could see the demons still approaching. They warped into more human forms as they did so, but that only bought us a little more time before they unleashed their full destructive power. With a gulp, I kept running.

We were faster on the sprint, but these demons were relentless. Gluttony or sloth demons, I guessed (probably sloth— gluttony demons were much fatter). We turned a corner to find a church down the street. Will called, "In there!" and the rest of my colleagues turned to follow. I hesitated, Ryan's shooting and Veronica fighting the angels still very fresh in my mind. But the demons were advancing on me and showing no signs of strain, while my lungs were protesting loudly. I glanced at the sign outside: *Catholic*. More organised than the Anglicans, hopefully unaffiliated with the band I'd previously had a run-in with. I'd have to take the risk that The One hadn't issued a general kill order on my head. Besides, the church *was* supposed to be a bastion of humanity, even if I was currently doubting that reputation.

I rushed inside to see my colleagues hurriedly talking with some armed men in riot gear with crucifixes around their necks. Each had an elongated red cross on a white field painted on one shoulder pad. My heart sank; it was apparent that the Knights Templar had modernised. Harriet was hurriedly explaining to them, "Look, you hate demons, right? There are a whole bunch coming right here, right now!"

The Templar's leader, a scarred man with a cross tattooed on his face, spoke in a matter-of-fact tone: "We have our orders; remain here until we're given the word. No going out and starting fights."

Harriet snapped, "They're just outside! Hardly picking a fight now, is it!?"

The Templar turned away. "I have my orders. Frankly, letting you shelter here is already bending them further than I'd like. I'm not outright breaking them. If they cross the threshold, then we engage. Not a moment before."

I peered out of the door to see a dozen brutish men lounging outside: the demons, crammed into human guise. Either the threat of the Templars or some efficacious sanctification on the church seemed to be holding the demons at bay for now, but they were obviously waiting patiently for a fight.

"Sloth demons. They've got nowhere to be," I groaned. I pulled out my phone. "Which means it's time to pull out the ace up my sleeve." I dialled and watched the phone ring.

Click. "Veronica Wainwright."

"V., long story short, I'm trapped in a church with some demons outside."

"Give me an address." After I did, she said, "I'll be there. Hold tight."

I turned back to the others. "Now we wait."

Will raised an eyebrow. "Who was that?"

"My girlfriend." I smiled.

Will gave me an incredulous look. "There are a dozen demons outside! And you called your *girlfriend!?*"

"She's a total badass!" I explained enthusiastically. "She once ——" I was about to bring up the fact that she had taken on two angels at once, before I realised the Templars may take exception to that particular feat. I opted for a less impressive one. "She cleared out a whole den of vampires, single-handedly! She wasn't even ready for that fight. A whole band of goons jumped her, so she grabbed one of *their* guns and started kicking ass! The vampire went for her, and she shot him clean through the chest!" I eagerly recounted the nightclub gunfight as we waited for her intervention.

Harriet shifted awkwardly. "You're sure about this? I don't want anyone else to get hurt. Maybe if we just find a corner, wait until sunrise …"

I dismissed the matter with a wave. "Nah, Veronica can handle these guys, just you wait."

Will sighed, pacing the pews awkwardly. The Templars took up positions around the church, watching both the demons and us. I settled down onto a pew. Harriet sat down next to me, tense as a bowstring. I wasn't entirely calm either, but that was more because of the Templars than the demons.

After a few more minutes, I heard some cackling outside from the demons, followed by the revving of a chainsaw and the sounds of a fight. I stood, rushed to the door and peered outside. I couldn't get a clear view of the fight from my angle, but I saw the demons resume their natural forms as they charged. It quickly turned into a storm of gore—a storm from which Veronica was the only thing to emerge, and she did so with a smirk, hefting a bloodstained chainsaw. "That's the last of 'em, honey!"

I emerged from the church and ran up to her. "Thank you!" I moved to hug her before realising she was covered head-to-toe in demonic ichor. I took an awkward step back. "Er, I'll … I'll let you find a shower."

Veronica smirked. "In a sec." She casually strolled up to the church, still hefting the gore-encrusted chainsaw.

The Templar squad leader was standing in the doorway, a frown on his face and a hand on his pistol. "Can I help you?"

Veronica's mood darkened. "I'm Thaleite, and I have a question: what the hell?"

The Templar's frown deepened. "We have our orders. I'm sure you can appreciate that."

"Orders to sit on your ass while demons are running around? You lie down and we have to pick up the slack!"

This didn't improve the Templar's disposition. "Say whatever you like. I had my orders, and I followed them to the letter. If there's a problem, your commanders can take it up with mine."

Veronica scowled but turned and left. I hurried after her, my colleagues following me in turn. When I was fairly certain we were out of earshot of the Templars, I turned to Veronica. "What was it, twenty guys after Ryan? And three angels? But demons start running around and …"

Will asked, "Wait, what are you talking about?"

I summed up, "Friend of mine, was enthralled to vampires. Some Anglicans tried to kill him, came bloody close to succeeding."

Veronica added, "Not the last time something like that happened. Not too long ago, I was on a joint op with the Templars—happens from time to time. Found some folks possessed by demons. Thought standard procedure for the Vatican was exorcism then trial, but the Templars went full scorched earth."

I cocked my head. "Thaleites and Templars working together?"

"The two of us have an arrangement. Bloody complicated, but I'm not a diplomat. But I'm wondering if the Vatican's holding up their side of the bargain."

Apparently the Thaleite's local base didn't have enough room for a gym, which was why Veronica (and, apparently, many of her squadmates) frequented one in the city. Veronica stopped using the absence of a 'regular' gym partner for pretence, both of us fully aware that I mainly showed up to watch Veronica's muscles ripple. Veronica had endured a small amount of ribbing from her squadmates over our apparent relationship. I wondered if they were envious.

One day, I was watching Veronica deadlift the kind of weight I figured would be used in astrophysics equations. After an impressive number of repetitions, she sat the weight down with a satisfied smile. "Hold on a sec, honey. I need the bathroom."

Her squadmate, Harry, quipped from an adjacent machine, "What, don't you want her to watch you there, too?"

Veronica aimed an offensive gesture in his direction as she headed back towards the locker rooms. Harry watched her leave. When she was out of earshot, he turned to me. "You know, she keeps a picture of you inside her combat webbing."

I flushed. "Does she? Gods, how on Earth did I get a woman like her?"

Harry released his hold on the machine and casually walked over to me. "To hear her talk about you, she's the one netting a girl out of her league. She's called you a puppy more than once."

My face turned a deeper red, and I squirmed from the second-hand praise. After a moment, Harry's expression turned serious. He leaned on the nearby wall and took a moment to choose his words. "Sarah, wasn't it? Veronica … might need your help, one day."

I looked at him, confused.

He explained, "Look, Veronica's the toughest woman I know, and I was a drill sergeant for a few years, and I beat a lot of people into shape. But she's not as tough as she thinks she is. She pushes herself hard, too hard."

I nodded. "I did see her try to wave off a medic after she was *literally* shot."

"That's not even the worst of it. She …" Harry glanced around, checking if anyone was listening "Look, I'm not supposed to tell you this, but it might be important one day. Some of our group are given … enhancements." He lifted up his singlet to reveal the same strange metal implant in his torso that Veronica had.

I leaned a little closer. "A 'pacemaker'?"

Harry gave a vaguely amused grunt. "I mean, it works as one, but it does a whole lot of other stuff. And this?" He flexed and tapped his muscles. "Let's just say there's a reason we don't do competitive sports."

Something clicked. I whispered, "Steroids?"

Harry shrugged. "Hell if I know what goes on in R&D, but it's serious stuff. The medics are constantly monitoring us and giving us instructions to make sure disaster doesn't strike. But you've seen how Veronica talks to them. They give her enough drugs to make Lance Armstrong jealous, she asks for more. She thinks that she can push through anything with just raw damn grit." Harry leaned down closer towards me. "One of these days, she's going to find her limit. And then someone will have to make sure she takes care of herself."

I nodded. "I will."

The promise was on my mind a lot; it wasn't hard to see how determined Veronica was in a fight. Even in training she pushed herself (and any gym equipment) hard. So, one night, as Veronica and I cuddled, I softly whispered, "Can I ask you something?"

"Anything."

"Why *did* you join the Thaleites?"

Veronica was quiet for a few moments. Then, she said, "Ever had a dog?"

I already had a guess where this was going. "Yeah, a border collie named Stella. She was a good girl, really smart."

"*Like little angels*, say people who don't know angels. They're better. So much better. But then ..." Veronica looked distant. "A demon." There was a long silence. "Don't think he was after anything. Just wanted an excuse to be violent. I saw it. I saw it happen, and I just snapped. Didn't even know about demons at the time. I just killed it. Bare damn hands. He called his friends. Killed them too. Hunted them. Thaleites saw my work and offered me the chance to do it full time."

I gently stroked her hair. "I get it. You're doing good work, I think." *Just be sure to make time to take care of yourself* was something I didn't have the courage to say.

Not long after, she dozed off, but even the short conversation was enough to keep me awake with the weight of all it meant. Veronica was a hero, fighting for humanity. A hell of burden. And here I was, able to support her. I was a lucky women. I had to admit, I'd wanted her from the first moment I laid eyes on her…

***

A year earlier

I didn't believe in love at first sight; I wasn't 12 anymore. But I did believe in *if-you-strangled-me-with-your-thighs-I'd-use-my-dying-breath-to-thank-you* at first sight, and that was my reaction to seeing the amazonian woman enter the gaming store. She was following Jake, a regular opponent of mine with messy hair and clothes always stained with machine oil. As much as I wanted to introduce myself, she was busy being shown around by Jake, and I wasn't so desperate as to interrupt. I returned to planning my miniature army.

A couple of minutes later, Jake got my attention. "Hey, Sarah!" When I looked up, I saw Veronica was standing by his side. "I, uh, meant to give Veronica a tutorial game, but I forgot I promised David a match. I don't suppose you could show her the ropes? I can loan you some of my models."

Oh fuck yes! "Sure, just give me a second to set up." It was on much shorter notice than I normally liked to do things, but I loved the game, and I certainly wasn't complaining about the chance to get to know this 'Veronica' better, so I quickly planned out how I'd teach the game as I set up the battlefield.

As I wrapped up, I said, "So, you're new to the game?"

Veronica was taking note of the way I set up. "Yeah. I'm new in town. Jake's my coworker. Haven't had all that much to do outside work, so he invited me. Enjoyed strategy games as a kid, so I figured it was worth a shot." She picked up one of the model futuristic tanks, carefully examining it. "So, what's the story behind these guys?"

Fictional lore: one of my favourite subjects. "Okay, *so* …"

***

The present

One late afternoon a couple of weeks later, I was heading home from a long day of wizardry when Ryan gave me a call. He sounded breathless. "Sarah? Do you know where Veronica is?"

"She was heading overseas for a few days—had a job to do for, you know, her security group. Is something wrong?"

Ryan paused briefly before answering. "I'm being followed. Two men in suits. Like the ones in the hospital."

My heart sank. I whispered, "Angels?"

"If that's what they were. Two of them. They don't look happy."

I shuddered. He needed a plan, fast, and I was his best bet. A half-baked research wizard. I had no damn chance, but I had to try. "Okay, try and find a crowd. Humans mess with angel's precognition; that'll slow them if they're after you. Where are you now?"

"City central, just passing by some office buildings. I'm cutting through a ———"

I heard a thump, then a yelp, and the line cut out. My already sinking heart plummeted. I immediately changed my route. I knew the city well enough to narrow down Ryan's location to within a couple of blocks, close enough for me to search. Ryan needed help. I was going to find him and ... *and do what?* I wasn't Veronica. I didn't stand a chance against an angel, let alone two. But I wouldn't forgive myself if I didn't try *something.*

I had a hand in my pouch of magical reagents and some mana built and ready as I looked around office buildings and into alleys. Then, I saw Ryan, sitting against a dumpster, talking to a concerned-looking woman in a trench coat. There were signs of a fight, but Ryan didn't seem seriously hurt. A dog with shiny gold fur was sniffing around the area. I peered around the corner.

The woman in the trench coat told Ryan, "Nothing broken, from what I can tell. But that was the last of their group;

you should be in the clear now. Just don't go talking about your … encounters in the club."

Ryan looked confused but not overly distressed. "Are you … Thaleites?"

The woman stood straight. "Just a good Samaritan." A 'good Samaritan' versus at least one, likely multiple, angels? I doubted it.

It was then that the dog noticed me, turning towards me and barking. As the woman peered in my direction, I stepped out into the open, preparing a wind-blast spell. The woman was on guard but not overtly hostile. "Can I help you?"

Ryan explained, "She's a friend."

The woman calmed. "Your friend was jumped by some thugs. He took a hard shove, but I don't think there's anything serious." The woman turned, whistled for the dog, and the two left.

I approached Ryan. "What happened?"

Ryan slowly stood. "They—the woman and the dog, and there was a third one—they jumped the two angels following me. It was a hell of a fight; you should have seen it. The angels completely ignored me as soon as the fight started. I think it was personal. The other trench coat guy went down, and he … disappeared. The same way the angels did."

I started analysing the situation. Even outnumbered, angels were a serious threat. The only reason the Thaleites had stood a chance in the hospital was because they were heavily armed and armoured (and, if what I'd heard was right, they weren't exactly baseline human either). But to take on angels without obvious equipment? And if one of them dissipated in the same way …

"Fallen angels."

Ryan blinked. "What?"

This was going to require some explanation. "Okay, so angels aren't really independent entities; basically, The One 'disconnects' parts of itself for a specific task. They're more like robots than people. But occasionally one goes rogue, getting free will. That's a fallen angel." When I started running through what I knew about fallen angels, something odd occurred to me. "But fallen angels are supposed to be very rare, and I've never heard of groups of them working together."

"Maybe it was just the one fallen angel and some, I don't know, cultists or something?" Ryan threw out the idea randomly, clearly aware he didn't know what he was talking about.

I sighed. "Maybe. I don't know. But … the other week, some demons chased me into a church. There was a whole squad of Templars there, but they didn't do anything."

"Templars? As in, the Knights Templar?"

"Yeah, they've modernised. The Vatican's monster hunters. Or so I thought." A dozen thoughts flicked around my mind, but they failed to cohere into anything useful. "Something strange is going on. I'll tell Veronica about it; she can pass it on to the Thaleites. But … anyway, let's get out of here."

As we walked away together, Ryan asked "You said something about angels, humans, and precognition?"

"Right. So, basically, while they're connected to The One, angels have a perfect understanding of every natural system and can predict how it'll act, but that stops as soon as a human gets involved." I explained. "Remember back in the hospital, the Thaleites fought them hand-to-hand? If you try shooting them, as soon as you pull the trigger, the angel knows exactly where the bullet's going to go. Fighting close quarters minimises the gap between the human making a decision and it having an impact, less room for the angel to manoeuvre."

"Right, so if we're in a crowd, all sorts of people and things the angels can't predict, that messes with them?"

I nodded. "Exactly. That, and acting in crowds tends to draw the authorities, and they have numbers and guns."

"Stick to crowds then. Will do."

Veronica and I were still very much enjoying the wargaming club. One night, I was setting up another match when I heard Veronica give an impressed whistle. I followed her gaze to where one of the game store's employees was unpacking a massive cardboard box, which contained an only-slightly-smaller cardboard box. The labels indicated it was part of the latest range of extra-large models for the wargame. Seeing our looks, the employee remarked, "Sorry, it's not stock. These things have to be ordered specially; each is $2000."

Eyes widened around the room. Veronica swore loudly, and my opponent remarked, "Who the hell spends that much on one model!?"

Another wargamer said, "It *does* look pretty cool."

I grumbled "They mark it up, they have to. There's no way that lump of plastic costs *that* much money.

My opponent chuckled. "Right. Might be easier to just make these ourselves."

That night, Veronica and I picked up our mediocre fast-food dessert, as had become something of a ritual. I could see Veronica was in a bad mood, and she said what was on her mind. "I was so damn hyped for those big models. But that much money? My job pays, but not *that* well."

I shrugged. "It's all marked up. The company knows everyone wants proper, branded models, and they charge accordingly." I smirked. "They don't know about conjuration magic though." At the look Veronica gave me, I giggled. "What? Did you really think I have the money to buy all those tanks? Nope, conjured. Have to shore them up once in a while, but *much* cheaper."

"And you've been holding out on me!?"

I honestly wasn't sure whether or not Veronica was genuinely offended. Regardless, I answered, "You never asked. But if you want models, I can make them. I could probably make one of those extra-large ones, with time."

Veronica's look of offence turned into a grin. "Oh, honey, you arrange me one of those, I promise you won't have to lift anything heavy ever again."

"I'm pretty heavy. Relatively speaking." I smiled coyly.

"No you're not. Let me demonstrate." With one hand holding her dessert, she effortlessly scooped me up using the other arm.

Chapter Six

"Hey Sarah, want to help me walk a dog?"

"Sure!"

Veronica had, a little abruptly, called me one day to ask that. Apparently the Thaleites had their own breed of dogs, but the kennels they used had been attacked by some malicious fey, so all the dogs had been moved to other bases while repairs were conducted and the handlers healed or replaced. Veronica's unit were taking turns caring for their furry comrades, and Veronica's turn was coming up to take one of the dogs for a walk.

I met her on a corner of one of the city's suburbs. She was wearing a simple tank top and cargo pants, and holding a leash. On the other end of the leash was a small terrier. One with short, gold-brown fur and a white stripe down his belly. It was excitedly running from place to place, sniffing everything that looked like it might one day be vaguely interesting. At least, until he noticed me, then he was straining against his leash to say hello, tail wagging like a propeller. Veronica smiled as she allowed him to approach. "Sarah, meet Rocket." Rocket happily leapt up (an impressive distance for such a tiny dog) and licked my face a few times before gravity forced him back out of range.

I giggled. "You know, when you mentioned your group had dogs ——" I was interrupted by Rocket leaping up again to get a few more licks in.

Veronica walked up to me, speaking quietly. "Thaleite terriers. Been breeding them for millennia. Apparently our forebears didn't want to see what happens when a dog tries to take on a vampire, but they wanted good trackers. Made these little guys: smart, curious, think they can take on a whole truck. Trained to sniff out the supernatural."

I knelt down and returned Rocket's affection with a vigorous scratch behind the ears. After gratefully accepting the scratches for a moment, Rocket lay down and showed me his belly. I took the hint, giving the happy dog some firm belly rubs.

After more pats than were practical but yet not enough to satisfy everyone involved, the three of us got to the actual purpose of the outing—getting Rocket some exercise. The little dog certainly enjoyed the walk, continuously running around and sniffing whatever caught his attention. He got himself tangled in his leash more than once. The excitable little fuzzball had both Veronica and I in high spirits; both of us laughed at his enthusiasm and curiosity, and we pondered if we might one day get a dog ourselves.

Then, Rocket's mood shifted. His tail dropped and his hackles rose as a faint grumbling emanated from him. Veronica frowned. "Something wrong, boy?" Rocket started prowling around a disused park we had found ourselves in, sniffing intently. Then, he reached an otherwise unremarkable spot on the ground and started digging.

I glanced at Veronica. "Should we …?"

Veronica shrugged. "I'm not normally a handler. Never got the training."

Rocket stopped digging after a moment, then he stood on the spot, paws close together. He barked quietly at us and stood still, clearly responding to some scent as he'd been instructed. As Veronica pondered the problem, I approached Rocket, knelt down and started feeling the mana currents around where Rocket was standing. "There's a spell here. Illusion magic, I think, but heavily degraded. Give me a second."

Dismantling someone else's spell could be a pretty complex task, but no-one had maintained this magic for quite some time, and I'd got into the habit of bringing along magical reagents whenever I went outside. I got to work while Rocket shifted impatiently, clearly expecting a reward for doing as he was told. After a moment's deliberation, Veronica caved, reaching into a pouch and handing Rocket a small treat, which he snapped up with a wagging tail.

I cast the right runes, and the dirt Rocket was standing on disappeared, revealing a rusty metal hatch. As the illusion magic faded from the æther, I noticed a different magic beneath it; something dark and polluted that made me shiver. "Hm … something's wrong here. Dark magic, I think."

Veronica crouched down beside the hatch. Rocket was still sniffing around but seemed on guard. I captured a mote of the ambient magic in a cage constructed of my will, held it with a summoned rune and examined it carefully. "Oh, this is definitely dark magic. Necromancy, I think."

Veronica tested the hatch. It was locked, but it opened with a snapping sound after Veronica gave it a firm tug (though a 'firm tug' from Veronica could rip a door clean off its hinges). As if in response, something *almost* human could be heard hissing in anger from below. All I could see was most of a rusty ladder, leading down into a dark corridor. Veronica frowned and handed me Rocket's leash. "Watch the dog for a second."

She leapt down into the darkness. I heard the sound of fighting. After a few minutes, she called, "All clear!"

"Was it undead? You might want to make sure they stay down," I called back.

There was a pause, the faint sound of something being crushed. "Now it's clear."

I scooped Rocket up in one arm a little awkwardly and carefully proceeded down the ladder. It was slow going; at least a quarter of the rungs were missing and half of those remaining were worryingly rusty. Luckily, it wasn't far down, a storey at most. Still, Veronica got a little impatient with my slow and steady progress, so she picked the two of us up off the ladder before carefully depositing us on the ground.

I conjured a small light in my hand to get a better look. We were in a small, circular tunnel leading to what looked like an open vault door. Beyond that, there was some sort of bunker with concrete walls. Undead of various varieties were scattered around, each with their skull crushed (by Veronica, presumably). Rocket was shifting anxiously, scanning for threats. Veronica led me into the bunker's interior. It looked like something built in World War II, with plenty of concrete, as well as old computers, but with more than a couple of supernatural elements—runes etched into the walls and exotic materials (and, of course, the freshly re-killed undead).

Veronica kicked one of the fallen bodies. "I think this guy was the ringleader. Necromancer. Pretty tough, actually. But also crazy."

"It's pretty common among older necromancers; existing in a state that's antithetical to life has … side effects." I examined the necromancer, a skeleton with flesh and robes hanging limply off, and found its grimoire, which was strapped to his belt in a holster common among wizards (though I had gradually been moving to a digital grimoire on my smartphone). I started to flick through. Contrary to the beliefs of the more conservative wizards and churches, there wasn't actually any problem with simply *knowing* about necromantic magics; it's just that most people who had it were those studying it, and those studying it were generally those intending to use it, and *that* caused problems. Having no interest in polluting the cycle of life and death myself, I casually flicked through, looking for any signs of what the necromancer was doing in here.

Veronica and Rocket, meanwhile, were examining the rest of the bunker. As I finished perusing the grimoire, Veronica came back. "Pretty big place. The necromancer had a small lab over there. Also found Church of England markings."

I mentally ran through what I knew of magical history. "This must have been built during the War of Three Truths."

Veronica looked thoughtful. "Heard of it but don't remember much, other than the fact that the name doesn't roll off the tongue all that well."

"Started between the World Wars. Pretty much everyone involved is, or was, shy about the details, but apparently The One turned away from humanity around the time we started dropping mustard gas on each other. The One was kind of cryptic at the best of times, so all the world's churches started bickering about why it happened and blaming everything from magic to technology to capitalism. Can't really blame them for that last one. Things got pretty brutal there for a time. Some time in the fifties, the churches all got together and hammered out a peace treaty that pretty much ended it," I explained. Then I added, "More or less."

I headed to the necromancer's lab and started browsing the notes there. As I did so, Veronica said, "I'll call a clean-up crew from the Thaleites. Don't want these bodies rotting here, especially if there's a chance they'll get back up." Her words seemed to remind her of the threat, and she took a second to smash the skull of a skeleton (already inanimate, heavily damaged and thoroughly dismantled).

She had to leave the bunker to get a signal. By the time she returned, I had a solid guess as to what the necromancer was doing. "It looks like the necromancer killed whoever set this place up and decided to use it as a hideout themselves. Then they started trying to invent a plan about building an army of the undead to conquer the world, but trying to do so without being detected kind of slowed them down. Guess that's why they left the door open. This place is pretty heavily warded—you wouldn't be able to cast much magic out with the wards at full strength."

"Any sign of any friends?"

"Not that I could see. Place should be safe."

Veronica nodded in satisfaction. "Well, unless there are any fancy magical things you want to look at, I think we're done here. My people should be able to find the place now there's no illusions."

A couple of weeks later, I woke up in the middle of the night to the distant sound of chanting outside my flat. Alarmed, I peered out through the window to see what was going on. Marching down the street were demons—at least two dozen, parading their true forms, exulting in the fear they caused. My heart sank. Veronica was out of the country for a few days on another operation for the Thaleites, so I couldn't call her for help, and the sentinels still communicated by carrier pigeon. With no better recourse, I barricaded my front door and placed reinforcing runes on all my windows. It wasn't much—I knew larger demons could break through walls—but it was all I could do.

While nothing happened to *me* that night, news spread about a string of assaults and break-ins along the street. I shuddered, thinking how I'd endured only out of sheer damn luck. I was increasingly convinced that I just wasn't safe in the city. Veronica had saved my life multiple times by this point, but she was only one woman, and she was helping the Thaleites defend far more people than just myself.

But I had an idea. As far as I knew, the necromancer Veronica had dispatched the other day had been working alone, which meant no-one else was using the bunker it had been holed up in. Which meant free real estate. Not the most comfortable place, but the same could be said of my flat, and at least the bunker was secretive and safe (and not currently owned by a bitch of a landlady).

The next time we spoke over the phone, I ran my idea past Veronica. "Hm. Bit of a fixer-upper, but doable. Want some help moving in?"

So, a few days later, Veronica and I returned to the bunker and started taking stock of the repairs that would be needed. It turned out there were several: the bunker's ventilation system needed extensive repairs, as did the electronics, and most of the furnishings were heavily rotted. The bunker was also impervious to electromagnetic signals of all kinds, meaning I'd have no internet or phone until I could come up with a solution. But those problems weren't beyond our ability to fix; the electronics weren't all that complicated, so I was certain I could call an electronically gifted friend, while Veronica had saved a mechanic from a hostile fey a while back and was sure she could pay him for some no-questions-asked repairs. I also knew a thing or two about information technology—enough that I had a plan as to how to connect the bunker to the digital world. So, we made some phone calls and got to work.

It was a project that took a couple of weeks. It took Veronica and I a few days just to scrub all the filth left by the bunker's previous undead inhabitants. Our contacts came through, and while the older infrastructure forced them to improvise when it came to parts, they managed to get everything functional and safe. It was expensive, but no more so than a couple of weeks' rent, so I considered it a wise investment. Meanwhile, with some signal-repeating magics and a few well-chosen lies to telecommunications companies, I managed to hook up the bunker's communication systems to the internet. While the place wasn't exactly aesthetically appealing, that was a problem heavily mitigated with the addition of a few posters and some nicer furniture. Veronica, of course, did the bulk of the heavy lifting.

Soon, I had a brand-new home, no less roomy than the flat I had been crammed into, and much safer. Veronica happily helped me haul all my stuff in before we broke in the new bed.

Over the next few months, our roleplaying group wrapped up our campaign, so Abby was starting another, in a steampunk system this time. I'd been doing some reading on the setting's lore, so we spent that evening discussing the future campaign and planning characters. When I floated the idea of building a big, burly super-soldier, Veronica immediately decided she'd play a wizard. Both of us tried, and failed, to keep a straight face.

As the session started to wrap up and we moved on to some more casual post-game chat, Abby's boyfriend, Carl—a man with the approximate proportions and body hair of a bear stocked up for winter—entered and joined in the conversation, casually leaning on the wall while he snacked on some chips. He wasn't part of the game, but no-one minded his presence, as he wasn't interrupting anything and was generally pretty nice.

Then, Carl abruptly doubled over. Abby looked at him, alarmed. "Honey? You alright?"

Carl didn't answer. Couldn't, probably. His body bulged and warped, bones rearranging, hair growing into a thick layer of fur. His clothes strained against his growth, finally failing and falling to scraps.

Abby shrieked in horror. Veronica stood, quickly positioning herself between Carl and the rest of us. Pat looked outside. "Yep, full moon. Okay, Sarah: Werewolves, what's the deal?"

"I don't think that's a werewolf!" I said, studying Carl's transformation. His nose did grow, but not into a canine snout. Instead, it morphed into something large and round. His ears shifted into a more animalistic structure, but not to canine points. His body, too, grew outright impressive levels of fat—again, not a predator's build. "That's a werewombat." At the looks the others gave me, I elaborated, "You know, like a werewolf. But a wombat."

Carl's transformation began to wrap up, leaving a disorientated wombat-man looking at us. Abby was as white as a ghost. Veronica was sizing Carl up, seeing if he'd be a threat, while Pat and Ryan were looking to me for advice. I provided. "Alright, everyone, stay calm; werecreatures generally aren't dangerous if you don't provoke them. Kind of like wild animals."

Carl examined us for a moment, sniffing the air. Then, he bent down and started scarfing down the chips he'd dropped on the floor. I sighed in relief. "Alright, he's just hungry. So long as we don't get between him and the food, we're good." I then addressed Abby in particular. "Though you might need some extra groceries."

Abby was still struggling to process what had happened. "He … it … I …" She raised a trembling hand towards Carl, who had finished most of the chips and was lumbering towards the pantry.

I walked over to her and knelt down. "Hey, hey. It's going to be alright. When morning comes, he'll turn back to normal, and in the meantime he's only really a threat to your wallet."

Pat seemed to have mostly calmed by now, but she still seemed concerned. "So how much of *Carl* is still in there?"

"That's kind of tricky," I explained. "The way the werekin curse works is it warps your soul, infecting part of it with primal power. The full moon boosts it, causing it to take over. Good news is that a lot of werekin work out how to 'stabilise' it, kind of like a meditation trick. It helps them stay lucid when transformed. I've heard there's a mob of werekangaroos in the city; one of them could teach him what he needs to know."

Ryan chuckled. "Shit, a werewombat? Werekangaroos? Not, I don't know, *weredingos*?"

I shrugged. "Don't feel too bad. I know a guy in Sydney who's a werehamster."

Pat laughed. "Fuck. Poor guy."

Abby stood slowly. "Wereanimals!? And you're just—you *know!?*"

I smiled awkwardly. "Uh, yeah, I'm a wizard. Veronica's a monster hunter, and that 'drug dealer' that got to Ryan? That was a vampire."

Abby blinked. "Wait wait wait, so does that mean Ryan's …?"

"A vampire? No, didn't get that far. Just a thrall, basically under mind control. But he's free now."

Ryan shuddered. He'd recovered from the worst of the enthrallment's effects, but the memories still haunted him.

Abby peered around a corner into the kitchen, where I could hear Carl feasting on the contents of the pantry. She slowly turned back to the rest of us. "So … what now?"

Veronica glanced around the corner as well. "Guess we just wait until morning. I can stay here tonight, if you want. If something goes wrong, I can handle him."

The next morning, I awoke to find Veronica had texted me a photo of werewombat Carl cuddling Abby, whose expression was of someone who had *no* idea what to make of the situation.

Word didn't always spread quickly among the supernatural community, as they hadn't grown attached to social media yet, but everyone quickly heard of a new major conference being held between the major supernatural powers regarding the recent uptick in demon activity, and the change in the behaviour of the holy forces. I was one of the first to know; Veronica had been assigned to the security detail for the Thaleite delegation, which meant she'd again be overseas for what could be weeks, or even months if things went bad. She and I made sure to spend plenty of time together in the time leading up to it.

Eventually, she left, and since she was travelling with her unit through classified routes, I couldn't see her off. The next couple of weeks were rough but not unbearable. My bunker gave me a level of safety, though it couldn't protect me when I left to do my job. I did my best to keep abreast of how talks were going, even if Veronica wasn't actually taking part, since progress meant she'd be back sooner. This made it difficult to hear that they were running into roadblock after roadblock.

Finally, after six long weeks, I received word from Veronica that talks were being put on hold a while, so she would get some time at home. When she returned, she headed straight to my bunker, and as soon as I let her in, she picked me up and carried me into the bedroom.

After I helped her handle the apparently *immense* amounts of frustration that had been building up during our time apart, she finally made some time to talk. I was too exhausted to say much, but Veronica had superhuman stamina.

"The talks didn't go well. Not allowed to say all that much, but apparently The One wants to beat the demons by cutting them off at the source: mortal sin." At the shocked look I gave her, she elaborated, "They're not going full genocide—at least, not yet. But apparently Ryan, and people like him, that's where it's starting. Us Thaleites did all we could, but I think we've only stalled things."

I'd caught my breath enough to ask, "Did any fallen angels turn up?"

"No, most there would have shot them on sight. Why?"

My oh-so-promising train of thought wasn't actually leading to anything all that useful. "Just thinking … Remember how Ryan ran into a couple? I think they might be starting to work together."

"Yeah, I've heard that too. The Thaleites have been using that as something of a bargaining chip, trying to convince the loyalists to focus on them."

I slowly sat up. "How many fallen angels are there?"

Veronica shrugged. "Anyone who knows isn't telling."

I felt like I had a puzzle just a few pieces shy of cohering into an image. More demons, fallen angels working together, churches becoming much more aggressive … it all pointed to *something* being gravely wrong.

But what?

Chapter Seven

It was just a couple of days after Veronica's return that Ryan gave me a call. "I've been trying to find out more about fallen angels, but I'm not sure what information's good and what isn't."

I shifted my grip on my phone. "Erm, not sure how much help I can be. I'm not an expert …" Then, I had an idea. "Hey, I just got a promotion that lets me takes guests into the Prismatic Spire's libraries. You can do your research there! I've got work to do there anyway."

"The Prismatic Spire?"

"The extradimensional headquarters of the Circle of Magi. Its libraries are *huge*. Makes them kind of hard to search through, since they haven't heard of computers, but it has to have what you're looking for!"

So, the next day, I took Ryan to the Spire. His eyes were as wide as saucers the entire time. I chuckled. "Happens to everyone, their first time."

I took him to the libraries and we split up, him searching for the texts on fallen angels and me doing some research for my arcane work. I made sure to check on him, which proved wise, as he wound up lost between the library's labyrinthine shelves. We took desks side by side and started reading.

The time it took to navigate the library alone ate up hours, and the two of us only had so much time, so after a while, we set aside our work for the day before returning the next. The library was an excellent place to study—nice and quiet, and across the street from an excellent cafe for when you needed a break.

Late on the second day, five heavily armed Templars entered the library, walking right up to Ryan. Every eye in the building was on them; Templars being armed and armoured in the Prismatic Spire was *definitely* in violation of one of the elaborate agreements established between the Circle and the Vatican in the wake of the War of Three Truths. The squad leader, who I recognised from when the demons chased me into the church, said, "Ryan O'Mannister? You're coming with us."

I stood angrily. "Hey! This is the Prismatic Spire, you have ——"

WHAM!

The next thing I knew, I was being revived by young woman wearing biomancer's sigils. "… fractures in the jaw, but I think I've got most of them," I heard someone say.

I found myself lying on the ground, amidst a somewhat contained commotion. Crouching over me was the biomancer and a man with a chiselled jawline wearing the silver shield pendant of the Circle's sentinels. "Sarah Torren? Did you witness what happened?"

My head was still throbbing. "Ngh … Templars, a whole squad with guns and everything." I sat up suddenly, looking around. "Wait, where's Ryan!?"

The sentinel stood. "The man with you? The Templars kidnapped him."

My heart raced. I quickly grabbed my phone, dialling Veronica's number. Luckily, she picked up. "Hey, honey. What's up?"

"Templars kidnapped Ryan!"

Veronica sounded outright confused. "Wait, what?"

I breathlessly explained, "In the middle of the Prismatic Spire—a whole squad! Remember that church the demons chased me into? I recognised one from there."

Veronica's tone turned from confusion to rage. "I'll pass this up the chain. I'll get him back, don't worry." *Click.*

Slowly, I stood. My head was finally starting to clear. The sentinel said, "If you don't mind, we'd like to get a statement from you." He led me to the nearby sentinel outpost, where I told a whole group of sentinels what had happened. I also filled them in on Ryan's history with the supernatural; the sentinels weren't saints, but they were more interested in other wizards than mortal affairs, so it was unlikely they'd target him.

As I finished, the captain, an older one-eyed woman, addressed me. "Well, I'll be having words with the Templars about just walking into the Spire armed to the teeth and hitting one of ours. But there's nothing I can do for your friend."

I started and stopped a dozen sentences, trying to figure out something to say to convince them to *do something*. One of the sentinels, a younger man with a scar running across his mouth, seemed to pity me. "Look, why don't I take her to the church? She knows where they're based. I can take her to demand compensation. Maybe you could use that as a bargaining chip to get him back."

The captain sighed. "Alright, but leave the matter of violating the Spire for later. That's something I'll be handling personally."

The sentinel nodded and turned to me. "Come on."

It was far from an ideal situation, but I had to make the best of it. The sentinel quickly changed from his wizard robes into a suit but kept his Circle and sentinel pendants on. I led him to the church, which looked deceptively more peaceful in the late afternoon light. We walked through the front door to find a seemingly ordinary priest talking with a woman in a suit who had a security guard by her side. The priest was saying, "This is a church, not a hotel. You must be mistaken."

A church that had an entire squad of Templars standing guard here not all that long ago, I thought to myself with a scoff.

The woman frowned. "I have good reason to believe ——" It was at this point the woman in the suit noticed us. Her gaze flicked to the sentinel's pendant. "Ah, I was wondering when you'd show. Quite quickly, it would seem."

The sentinel's brow furrowed. "And you are …?"

The woman held up an ID card. "Kaylee Koren-venn, Thaltech security."

"Are you here for Ryan?" I asked.

Kaylee nodded. "Indeed. As previously mentioned, I have good reason to believe he's here."

As the priest continued to deny it, I had an idea. I gave Ryan's phone a ring. Faintly, in the distance, I heard Ryan's ringtone, followed by someone yelling at someone else for their incompetence. Kaylee glanced at me. "Mr O'Mannister's phone, I presume?"

I nodded, grinning at the priest. A moment later, the Templar squad leader and one of his men marched out from a back door. Dismissing the priest with a gesture, he turned to the four of us. "Look, I don't know what you want ——"

I interrupted, "You kidnapped my friend!"

The Templar said in a matter-of-fact tone, "I'm under orders. Now, turn around and leave."

The sentinel and Kaylee both started to talk at the same time. Both paused, and Kaylee gestured for the sentinel to continue. He did so. "You marched into the Prismatic Spire, in gross violation of the Treaty of New Orleans, and struck a member of the Circle. Now, my superiors will be speaking to yours about the former offence, but I'm here to demand compensation for fracturing a Circle member's jaw."

I added, "But if you let Ryan go, I'll drop the whole thing."

The Templar looked to be getting frustrated. "I can't! I have orders!"

Kaylee said, "Then I ask for a meeting with your commanding officer. If you can't guarantee the safety of Mr O'Mannister, then my organisation will take quite serious offence."

The Templar growled, then spoke into a radio. "Sir? A Thaleite and a sentinel are out front. They want our man, and they are getting insistent … Yes, sir." He turned back to us. "He'll be out momentarily."

Everyone else nodded, Kaylee much more patiently than the sentinel or myself. A few moments later, a man in an impeccable suit with square sunglasses walked out. "Thaleites and Circle mages, the man you call Ryan O'Mannister has been consorting with the enemy."

I blinked. "Demons? No way! He'd never do that."

The man in the suit said, "Fallen angels, specifically."

I frowned. "He was researching them!"

The man turned to me. "You know of this?"

I decided to be vague on the details. "He wanted to know more, so I took him to the library."

Recalling the event in the future, I would later guess that the man in the suit took me to be an accomplice of Ryan's and sought to take me into custody. In that moment, all I could figure out was that someone drew a gun, in response to which everyone else drew their guns, leading to everyone firing on everyone else for drawing guns—and that's how the fight started.

My danger-sensing ring was still working as needed, which was lucky, because I needed the split-second warning to pump enough mana into my wards to absorb the bullet. Luckily, most of the other bullets flying around were aimed at the more threatening people in the room, so I had space enough to duck for cover behind a pew. Kaylee did so as well, saying into an earpiece, "Green light! Green light!"

Then, one of the walls exploded. A titanic armoured figure strode into the room, holstering a grenade launcher and trading it for a machine gun. My ears rang as a hailstorm of lead filled the room. I ducked down, plugging my ears to drown out the deafening noise.

My curiosity was strong enough for me to peer out from behind the pew at the fight. The sentinel was already heavily wounded, leaning on a pillar with worryingly bright-coloured blood oozing out. Kaylee seemed unhurt but eager to stay out of the fight, and her security guard seemed to have taken a hit. Fortunately for them, the Templars had turned their attention to the armoured newcomer, and it was attention they could take. Bullets bounced off their armour with metallic *pings*, and the damage done didn't look serious. Their weapon, too, looked like the kind of gun it took a whole team to crew, but this fighter handled it with the ease of any rifle, cutting down the Templars in a second with bullets that went straight through their cover. During a brief pause in the gunfire, I could hear the thrum of motors. My eyes widened; had someone developed *power armour!?*

The man in the suit rushed towards the armoured figure, somersaulting over a hail of lead into a close-quarters fight. I gulped; he was probably another angel. The angel's fists, even with enhanced strength, could only do so much against the heavy armour, but that wasn't the angel's tactic: he was trying to get a point-blank pistol shot, with the hope that the close range would allow penetration. The armoured warrior didn't just stand back and allow that to happen, turning the massive gun into a club and engaging the angel. The warrior was much stronger and only a little slower.

It was then that more Templars emerged from the back. They aimed their rifles at the armoured figure but held their fire, clearly not wanting to hit the angel. The angel said something I couldn't hear over the tinnitus, and the Templars started firing single shots, which the angel dodged successfully. The armoured figure staggered back but was able to fire a burst from their weapon that drove the Templars to cover, if only for a precious second. The angel moved back into melee, but the warrior saw this coming and grappled him, using the momentum to throw him towards the Templars.

The angel effortlessly rolled into a landing, but the warrior was just trying to get him away from everyone else; after doing so, they switched to their grenade launcher. Angels were inhumanly agile, but the whole point of a grenade was that you didn't need to land a direct hit. The blast shredded the angel's suit and drew a disgusting amount of blood, as well as taking out a number of the Templars. A second blast finished the angel off.

The warrior removed their helmet. It was Veronica. She examined a deep scratch in her visor left by a lucky bullet, before discarding it. She looked at me. "Wasn't expecting you to be here, Sarah. You good?"

There were a million emotions dancing in my head, but I settled on one to process first. "Is it weird that I find you kind of sexy in all that armour?"

Kaylee cleared her throat. "Erm, I'm not sure that was all of them, and we still have a missing man …"

Veronica swapped back to her machine gun. "Right, you can fawn over how heroic I look later." She started advancing towards the back of the church, scanning for enemies.

As I contemplated whether or not to follow her, Kaylee's guard checked the sentinel. "He's dead."

It was sad news; I didn't know him, but he had tried to help and died for it. I felt a stab of anger at the Templars, and a little guilt, as he was here on my account. I came to a decision: my danger ring and wards had proved to be protection enough against stray bullets and snap shots, so as long as I kept my head down, I could follow Veronica (at a distance) without being in *too* much danger. Besides, it was plainly obvious that she was the more threatening of the two of us. So, I followed her into the back, slowly peering around corners before I turned them.

I heard a few more deafening rounds of gunfire, followed by the heavy stomping of Veronica's massive armour. Peering into the next corner, I saw Veronica walking away from another cluster of Templar corpses. I almost felt sorry for them; I'd seen firsthand what Veronica was capable of when unarmed, so when she was clad in futuristic armour and holding massive weapons, she'd be nigh-invincible.

She kept moving, methodically sweeping the church until she found a hatch in the ground. She briefly checked it, finding it locked. She then ripped it open as casually as one would open a can of soup. She descended. I heard another round of gunfire, followed by some talking (difficult to make out, as I suspected by this point that the gunfire had permanently impaired my ability to hear). Again looking around to make sure no more Templars were sneaking up on me, I slowly walked down the stairs.

I saw a small underground chamber, bare concrete—a stark contrast to the gilded ground floor. The chamber had a small armoury to one side and various holy artefacts in the back. To the other side was a cage, containing Ryan. He was tied to a chair and looked to be badly beaten. Veronica was holding a Templar at gunpoint. "Open the cage," she scowled at him.

The Templar said, "I don't have the key."

Veronica snarled. Then, still aiming the machine gun at the Templar with one hand, she bent open the bars to the cell. So as not to give the Templar any chances for trickery, I said, "I'll get him!" and ran through the gap towards Ryan.

He muttered, "Never going to nightclubs again."

I chuckled nervously. Inspecting his bindings, I called to Veronica, "Got a knife?"

"He should have one." Veronica inclined her head towards a nearby Templar corpse.

It was then that one of the relics in the back of the room, a large golden scripture-inlaid ring, began to glow. Light gleamed at its centre, where space warped into a portal. A figure emerged—

an elegant ivory idol with the proportions of a human torso surrounded by spinning rings, each inlaid with wings and eyes. An angel in its true form.

One of its rings stopped spinning as an eye focused on me. Veronica dived between me and it as the eye glowed and fired a blast of searing light. Shielding her head with her armoured hand, she fired a quick burst, forcing the angel to shift positions, which it did with alien speed. Seeing the danger, I abandoned my search for a knife and quickly conjured a flame to use on the bindings. After it ate through enough of the fibre, I hurriedly tore the bindings off.

The angel switched tactics, slipping back through the portal. As Veronica tried to line up a shot, the portal closed. Veronica was halfway through muttering something about cowardice when the portal opened just long enough for the angel to fire a blast through. Veronica quickly ducked, but she was still left with a nasty-looking burn across her cheek. The portal closed again before Veronica could return fire.

Ryan, meanwhile, was free, but he barely made it a step before he collapsed. He looked up at me pleadingly. "Can't … walk …" Not sure what else to do, I dragged him to shelter between the armoury's shelves, hoping that no-one would be stupid enough to fire wildly at a cluster of explosives.

Veronica had taken cover beside the portal, which continued to open and close for the angel to fire through. Veronica swore loudly. "Bastard!"

Peering between the racks of guns, I examined the portal, attuning my senses to the aether. I examined how the currents of magic flowed into reality as the portal opened and closed, studying how the portal was structured. I realised something. "Veronica! I might be able to hold it open." I didn't have time to point out that doing so would be very dangerous.

Veronica switched to her grenade launcher and gave me a nod, brow furrowed in determination. With the angel focused on Veronica, I slipped out and rushed to the side of the portal. The enchantments behind the portal were powerful but surprisingly simple, at least as far as such spell constructs went. I saw a small flaw in how the magic flowed. With an incantation, I wove my will into the spell and tore the gate between realities open. It was intense, something I could only hold for a second, but a second was all Veronica needed. She fired a barrage of grenades through the portal.

Veronica was grinning as my grip on the magic slipped and the portal closed. "Think I got him!"

I was about to congratulate her on a job well done when I felt a surge of strange magical energies, like a hot shiver across my whole body. I had a terrible feeling. "Something's changed," I said quietly.

Veronica looked at me quizzically. "What?"

"Maybe you blew up something you shouldn't have … we'll find out soon enough. Let's get Ryan out of here."

Veronica holstered her weapon and carefully picked Ryan up. She glanced at me. "Keep an eye out for me, puppy. I don't want to get jumped if there are any more Templars lurking around."

We managed to exit the church without further incident. We walked outside.

And saw the sky turned blood-red.

I felt like my heart was in freefall. I was silent. All Veronica could say was, "That ain't good." After a pause, she started jogging down the street, beckoning for me to follow, though with her already massive stride enhanced by the armour's motors, I had to sprint to keep up. She turned into an alley, where we found Kaylee and her guard by a pair of vans. Kaylee asked, "What the hell happened in there?"

Veronica sighed. "I … fired a whole bunch of grenades into heaven. Angels were shooting at me ——"

Veronica's armour started beeping just as Kaylee and her guard started focusing on their earpieces. Veronica hurriedly set Ryan down inside one of the vans before flipping open a panel on her gauntlet and pressing a button. I could faintly hear a woman's voice from a radio inside. "International command. All Thaleite assets are raised to black alert. I say again, all Thaleite assets are raised to black alert. Abort non-critical missions and report to your posts. Further orders incoming."

The three present Thaleites all had eyes as wide as saucers. Kaylee was the first to speak. "I've never even heard a black alert before."

Veronica's shoulders slumped. "I have—only once. And all of us? *All* of us?" She gritted her teeth. "I'll grab my helmet. We can dump Ryan at the hospital, but then we have to report in. Something bad's going on."

I said, "The portal to the Prismatic Spire isn't far. I'll see what's going on in the Circle. If I learn anything, I'll text you."

Veronica stepped into the van, the suspension visibly shifting under her armour's weight. "Sounds like a plan. And … be safe."

"You too."

There wasn't anything immediately wrong or unusual in the Prismatic Spire, but I did hear a lot of chatter between my fellow mages, all of whom were deeply concerned about a worldwide shift in mana, as well as the fact that the sky had turned blood-red. I wasn't terribly sure where to start, but I figured that if I headed back to the sentinel outpost, I could tell them what had happened in the church.

I walked in and told their captain everything. The death of one of their own was obviously hard news to take, but they didn't interrupt.

"Then, I had an idea: I could force the portal open, which would let Veronica return fire," I said, reaching the climax of my tale.

At that, the captain's eyes widened. "Wait … did you kill an angel in heaven?"

I blinked. "Um, Veronica might have. She fired a few grenades through the portal."

The captain buried her face in her hands. "The death of a celestial in their realm is the ultimate violation."

I frowned. "Then maybe they shouldn't have beaten my friend!"

The captain looked at me. "You don't get it! Killing an angel in heaven starts the apocalypse!"

"Oh … Well, that could be better advertised."

"Most people don't kill angels at all!"

"The angel was trying to kill us!"

"She fired a grenade launcher into *heaven!*"

"The angel trying to kill us was hiding there—and we didn't know!" I sighed. "Give me a second. I should let Veronica know …"

She answered on the first ring. "Veronica Wainwright, make it fast."

"Turns out killing an angel in heaven sets off the apocalypse."

"You'd think that'd be better advertised."

"That's what I said!"

Veronica grunted. "Alright, I'll pass this up the chain. Gotta go. I have a feeling there'll be a lot of asses to kick real soon."

"Give 'em hell, V." *Click.* After a short period of grim silence, I asked the sentinel captain, "So … what do we do?"

The captain stood straight. "*We take cover* is what we do. Hold the Spire at all costs. Other than that … hope the demons are more interested in mortals than mages."

"I—are—can't we do *something*!?" I stammered.

"No."

I wasn't ready to accept that, so I headed straight to the library and found everything I could about the apocalypse. Unfortunately, the answer turned out to be *not much*. The Circle of Magi had been trying to keep out of The One's business for most of its existence, and that meant information about it was light on the ground. Worse, as soon as word of the coming apocalypse spread, a number of the library's staff left in order to ensure the safety of their families. I at least found a general briefing on the nature of the apocalypse: Upon the defilement of heaven, the barriers between realities would be massively weakened and many of the rules abandoned, allowing supernatural creatures to arrive on Earth en mass, to the point that demons could launch a full-scale invasion of Earth. At least Veronica would be enjoying herself—or so I hoped. The barriers between the worlds of the living and the dead being fractured would also cause a massive spike in the number of undead. The stability of magic would also be reduced, causing older or disregarded spells to fail in potentially spectacular ways.

As I was researching, I got a call from Pat. "Hey, Sarah? Uh … sky's turned red way too early. Is that a, you know …"

There was no dancing around the issue. "It's the apocalypse."

"Seriously?" Pat's neutral tone made it obvious he had no idea how to process what I'd just said.

I'd somehow completely disengaged from my rising panic and begun to look at the situation from a problem-solving lens. "Yeah. Look, I'm going to be honest: I don't know what to do. For now, gather food and water, get yourself and your folks somewhere safe."

Pat grunted awkwardly. "What do you mean by 'safe'?"

"Good question. You want either somewhere with a good food and water supply, somewhere away from tempting demon targets, or somewhere solid. In fact, all of those, on the off chance you can get that. Also, avoid cemeteries. People might not be staying dead." Something in my brain clicked. "Ryan's in hospital —" then something else "—but Veronica took him there, so hopefully she'll dispatch anything from the morgue."

Pat sounded like his distress was starting to break free. "I don't know anywhere like that! My place is filthy, and my folks are in the suburbs."

Time for my good deed for the day. "I know a place. It's not got solid food stocks, so you'll have to bring your own."

"I'll bring everything I can carry."

After stocking up on what supplies I could from the small stores in the Spire, I headed straight to the bunker. By some stroke of luck, the bus services were still running, and I managed to get to the edge of the suburbs before the one I was on got stuck in traffic. Given that it was jammed to a standstill, I decided to get out and walk; crossing the road was remarkably easy with none of the cars able to move.

As I walked through the suburbs, my fear steadily built. I could hear dozens, maybe hundreds, of sirens in the distance, and even gunfire. My heart beat anxiously. I kept expecting a demon or other creature of darkness to burst from a shadowy corner. I scanned the area constantly for potential threats. At least my fear allowed me to push myself harder than I normally did, and I covered the ground in good time.

I met Pat in the park, along with his mother and sister. His mother, Willow, was aptly named. His sister, Katey, had inherited a good deal of her mother's genes, including her tall and slender build. Pat had clearly listened to me; all three were laden with bags of supplies. Pat sighed in relief as I approached. "Sarah! I was worried something had happened to you."

"Stuck in traffic, had to walk. Come on." I showed them into the bunker, a logistical exercise due to the sheer amount of stuff we were carrying. Nevertheless, we all made it inside without incident. Fortunately, the bunker had been built to store large quantities of supplies for an extended period, so there was plenty of room. Beds proved to be a more difficult resource to provide, as I'd removed most of the bunker's cots (not that they were in acceptable condition anyway) and only installed room for myself, but we managed to stretch the various cushions and blankets I had around to get everyone to acceptable levels of comfort.

Finally, I had a chance to relax. I slumped back on my bed, feet aching. Social media was already aflame with news of demon and undead attacks and the authorities' desperate attempts to establish order within the chaos. I thought about Veronica, out there, fighting those creatures. I wondered if even she was enough to make a dent in what was to come.

I thought about the rampant death and destruction.

I thought about the world ending.

I wondered if I'd have another chance to be happy again.

I cried.

An hour later, I still lay on the bed. My tears were spent, for now, but my heart was still in a dark place. There was a knock on the bedroom door and Pat entered. "Hey, we found your stash of board games. We don't have much else to do, do we?"

He was right. So, we sat down and played. My stash wasn't all that large—board games weren't my favourite pastime—but it was better that lying down and lamenting the end of the world. Pat and his family were decent enough company.

The next morning, breakfast was meagre. After we ate, Willow asked, "So, what's the plan?" In response to the quizzical look I gave her, she elaborated, "So, are we just going to sit here until …?"

I sighed and leaned back in my seat. "Good question. Honestly, I have no damn idea. I don't know how things are going to shake down. Angels could burn the world, or demons, or maybe everything will blow over … I don't know."

I saw something like determination in Pat's eyes. "Then let's worry about supplies lasting until whatever happens happens. We're going to need more food and water. Any way your magic can help with that?"

I looked thoughtfully at my empty bowl. "Good question. I have a knack for conjuration, but conjuring *nutrients* is actually really complicated, especially because I can't actually create matter—well, there's the whole $e=mc^2$ thing, but c^2 is a massive number. Anyway, when I conjure something, it's actually just solidified mana, which only exists so long as a spell construct can maintain it, which when you're making food will have to be as long as your body is using it. I suppose I could try, but I'd have to go back to the Prismatic Spire to do research, and the nearest portal to the place is a drive away."

"I could go with you," Pat said. "The two of us survived the nightclub, right?"

"That's because Veronica was there," I pointed out.

Willow suggested, "Alright, why don't we just wait a day, see how things pan out? Then we can just peer out, see what's going on. Then we can make more plans."

Pat sighed impatiently. "That … I guess. I just don't like doing nothing."

"Is there anything we can do?" Katey asked quietly.

I considered that problem. "Short of signing up to the army, or the Thaleites …"

Pat stood. "Then that's what I'm going to do. Veronica's with them, so they can't be half-bad."

"I'm not sure you can exactly just walk up to their base. Hell, you can't just walk anyway, and I don't even know where they're based," I said in a matter-of-fact tone.

Pat sat down, deflated. "I … ugh. Alright, we stay down for a day. Then we figure something out."

We spent most of the day just conserving our energy. Late in the evening, not long before I was about to try and get some sleep, the bunker's intercom buzzed. I flicked the button to answer. "Hello?"

"Sarah? It's me, Veronica."

My heart soared. "Just a second!"

I rushed over to the bunker's door and opened it. I saw Veronica standing there, still in her power armour, holding her helmet by her side. It was noticeably damaged and covered in demonic ichor. I didn't care. I threw myself at her, enveloping her in a hug (though with the bulk of her armour on top of her already immense size, I couldn't get my arms all the way around). Veronica smiled widely, gingerly stroking my hair with a gauntleted hand. She spoke quietly, "Hey, puppy."

I stepped back into the bunker. "Come in, come in!"

Veronica did so, unusually muted. "Not staying for long, gotta get back into the field soon. But command insisted I take a break for a bit, so I figured I'd check on you."

"Things are … so far, so good. Pat and his folks are staying with me; we've got enough supplies for a week, maybe two." As the ichor sinking into my clothes began to make itself known, I shifted uncomfortably. "But how are things topside?"

Veronica's voice had no more animation than her body language. "We're fighting. It's still hell on Earth up there, but there are safe points here and there. Can't tell you much more, but if everything goes to plan (big *if*, I know), we should have some shelters established in the next couple of days." She then seemed to have an idea, reaching into a pouch on her pack and pulling out a bundle of food. "Here, I've got some extra rat packs. Tastes like shit, but better than starving."

I took it but hesitated a moment. "You sure you've got enough?"

"Yeah, yeah. Don't worry about me."

Pat emerged from the bunker's bathroom. "Veronica! Hey, could you get me signed up with the Thaleites?" When Veronica's expression shifted to mild surprise, he added, "Come on, I don't want to just sit here doing nothing!"

Veronica smiled, though there was an undercurrent of sadness. "Sure, we could use everyone that can hold a gun. Just …" Veronica hesitated, something clearly weighing on her mind.

Katey, who'd been peering around from a corner, asked, "Is something wrong?"

Veronica said, "I lost a friend today. One of my squad— Harry was his name. Demons got onto our flank. Big ones, and …" There was a solemn silence. Then, I saw Veronica clench her fists. "I can't stay. Pat, you still keen on fighting? Real chance you won't be coming back."

Pat seemed to just now process the risk he was about to take, but he nodded with the subtle nervousness of someone who knew they didn't understand the nightmare they were walking into but believed it would be worth it, for others if not himself. Willow and Katey looked at him, then each other. Neither of them *wanted* him to go, but nor could they object after seeing how desperate he was to contribute.

Veronica took a deep breath. "Alright. The base will have everything you need, but if you want to grab any small mementos, now's the time."

Pat gave a nervous laugh, slinging his bag over his shoulder. "Was already only carrying the essentials." He thought for a moment. "Yeah, I've got everything."

Willow suddenly stepped forward, wrapping her son in a warm and tight hug. Pat reciprocated, both keenly aware this could be the last they saw of each other. Katey joined them. After a sad moment that was both long and far too short, Pat pulled away, his expression one of resolve. Willow whispered, "I love you."

Pat gripped his bag. "Love you too." Then, he turned to Veronica and gave her a nod. Veronica nodded back and led him out. Katey, Willow and I watched the pair climb back up to the surface. Then, I closed the bunker door. The door clanking into position sounded terminal.

A couple of days passed in the bunker. Katey and Willow took an interest in my wargaming, so I taught them how to play and watched as they had a few matches against each other. My conjuration magic managed to provide terrain enough, and it succeeded in keeping our minds off the progressing apocalypse for a while.

I'd had the bunker's radio systems repaired, and apparently some people had the equipment to broadcast. Word from the authorities was foremost; they'd apparently managed to establish some shelters (though Katey, Willow and I agreed that, for now, the bunker was probably more secure). There were also broadcasts from religious groups, some promising shelter in their churches, others promising damnation for infidels, and some promising both.

Finally, Veronica returned to the bunker. Katey let her in while Willow and I made dinner. She wasn't wearing her power armour this time and was instead dressed in military fatigues, though she was still armed, this time with a pistol and combat knife. With her lighter clothing, it was easy for me to see a number of bloodstained bandages. Despite those, she was grinning. "Hey, puppy!"

I quickly set down my utensils and rushed to give her a warm hug. "V! I'm glad you're still alright."

Veronica returned the hug. "Can stay for a whole night tonight. Medics insist on me resting that long."

"Of course they do! Look at you, you've been through hell, and I'm not sure whether or not that's literal!" I exclaimed, withdrawing and gesturing to her bandages.

Veronica sighed, walking towards the kitchen. "I know it's kind of sudden, but do you have anything nicer than rat packs to eat?" We did, and while it might not have been exactly practical, I'd been miserable for days, so I allowed myself to do something that would make me feel good, even if only for a moment. We managed to make something out of the fresh food that was still good, much to Veronica's joy.

As we ate, Willow asked, "Have you seen Pat?"

Veronica shook her head. "He was shipped off to a training camp. Normally, we spend a good couple of months getting folks ready to fight, but the apocalypse might speed things up a bit." After a brief silence, Veronica added, "Look, I'm not going to lie and say he'll be fine; this shit is hard. But we Thaleites look after our own. So let us worry about him."

Willow shook her head. "I can't do that."

Veronica smiled sadly. "Yeah, suppose you can't."

Afterwards, I talked Veronica into a match of our wargame, with her borrowing my models. I was expecting a solid win, since she wouldn't be as used to my army, but she ended up beating me soundly. Willow and Katey watched, not really following but glad of the distraction.

Night came, and Veronica and I lay on the bed. Little was said or done. But we were there, together. I knew that, come morning, she'd be gone, marching off to fight for the fate of the world. But that made it all the more important to cherish these moments between the apocalypse.

A week later, the authorities announced over the radio that most of the demons and their followers had been beaten back from the city, at least for now. With little word from the religious factions, and our supplies running low, I decided to take the risk of venturing out. I hoped to learn the secrets of food conjuration from the Prismatic Spire's libraries, and I also planned to stop by the shelter the authorities had set up to see if I could convince them to part with some food.

Miraculously, Willow's car had endured the carnage with only a few dents on the side, perhaps from something slamming into it during the innumerable fights. A quick examination revealed it was in good enough condition to drive, so Willow gave me a lift.

It was strange, driving through the ruined city. There was no traffic on the road, though Willow still drove slowly and carefully. I couldn't see a single building without a smashed window or door. There wasn't any power in the city, not a single traffic light or streetlamp. It was eerie seeing them all black.

We reached the portal to the Spire. I exited the car and Willow drove off to see how her house had fared. As I entered, I found that the Spire, at least at first glance, hadn't been hit hard by the apocalypse. But soon after leaving the portal, I was confronted by a sentinel, a large, burly man with overly styled facial hair. "You! Are you under any contracts?"

"What?"

The sentinel marched into my personal space. "Are. You. Under. Any. Contracts?"

I took a step back nervously. "I-I have a job—or had, maybe—in a research cabal."

"Are you giving me lip?! I'll detain you!" the sentinel yelled.

As I stammered out a response, another mage approached from a nearby street. I recognised Martin Dorrin-Wells, a Circle politician, and senior Green Hand. "Stand down, sentinel! That's an order!"

The sentinel turned to argue, and the pair stared at each other for a moment. Finally, the sentinel sulked off. Dorrin-Wells muttered, "Bully!"

I nearly laughed in relief. "Mr Dorrin-Wells! Thank you so much!" I offered him my hand, and he gave it a firm shake.

"Please, call me Martin," he said. "And no need to thank me—the sentinels have been overstepping their authority ever since the apocalypse started."

"That bad? I've been, uh, hiding in a bunker for the last week or so …" I rubbed the back of my neck sheepishly.

Martin snorted in amusement. "Probably smart. Things have been pretty bad; the Circle's about to tear itself apart. Everyone's selling their services to the various factions, and people have started thinking that means they have to 'claim' the Spire for their employers."

"Truth be told, I *have* been thinking of signing up to the Thaleites," I mumbled.

"Thaleites? Well, you could do a lot worse," Martin remarked.

The subject brought out a light smile in me. "My, uh, girlfriend is actually a Thaleite. She's probably out there right now, killing demons." I decided to not mention the fact that she was quite likely the one that started the apocalypse in the first place (hell, I'd had a hand in that).

Martin raised an eyebrow. "Really? Well, I wish her luck. I think the Thaleites can be reckless at times, but at least they're trying to protect people."

I turned to leave. "Anyway, I've been meaning to research food conjuration. See you around."

After a couple of hours, I'd found a promising research lead, but it'd take time to follow up, maybe days. I borrowed a couple of the books so I could do what research I could from the safety of my bunker, and I also took the chance to buy what supplies I could carry from the nearby stores (though I noticed prices had jumped significantly).

When I left the portal, I found Willow in her car waiting for me. I entered, loading what I had into the back seat. As I sat in the front, I asked, "How was it?" Willow simply stared ahead blankly, cheeks tear-stained.

After a moment of silence, I simply said, "Oh …" What else was there to say?

We headed to the shelter. It had been established in what had once been a school. It was fortified with sandbags, and armed soldiers were scanning the area from the perimeter. One waved us into the nearby parking lot. The place was packed with refugees of all stripes, people sitting by every wall and corner. The school's canteen was being used to distribute rations, and Willow and I were soon shepherded into a lengthy line. We were only given enough for one meal, but at least that was one meal saved in the bunker.

As we sat and ate, I heard a delighted cry from the side. "Sarah!" It was Abby, running towards me happily. Before I could process what was going on, she wrapped me in a hug. When she released me (still stunned), she kept holding my shoulders. "I hadn't heard anything from you! I was so worried!"

My brain managed to finally assemble an appropriate response to the situation. "I'm … I'm fine. I've found a place to hole up in. I have this—" I glanced around at everyone nearby "—safe place. Oh, Abby, this is Willow, Pat's mum. She and Pat's sister are staying with me."

Abby greeted Willow with a nod. "Pleasure to meet you! Speaking of Pat, have you heard from him?"

"He decided to sign up with the Thaleites, Veronica's order of monster hunters. Veronica took him to their base, and they shipped him off to a training camp. But how are you doing?"

Abby laughed with a million half-realised emotions. "Oh, it was terrifying! Those *things*—demons, they're being called— one came at me, but Carl, he's managed to get a lot of the werewombat thing down, so he grew massive and just started thumping them! It was … honestly, gross. Were-things can only be killed with silver, right?"

"Kinda. They can be killed with ordinary bullets, but you'd need an awful lot to overpower their regeneration, which silver disrupts. And werewombats would be even tougher than most werekin," I explained.

Abby nodded. "Okay. Well, he was tough enough for them." A pause. "Hey, have you heard anything from Ryan?"

I shook my head. "Veronica rescued him from some Templars just before the apocalypse; he'd been beaten pretty badly, so Veronica sent him to the hospital. That was just when the apocalypse was starting."

"Well, I heard the hospital is still working. Maybe he's alright!" Abby's tone was optimistic, something that was rare in such a crisis.

I turned to Willow. "Could we drive past the hospital and check on him?"

She agreed, so after lunch, we headed there. The authorities had set up a fortified perimeter around it, and Willow and I found ourselves having to answer a number of questions for a paranoid (and heavily armed) guard. Eventually, he was satisfied, and we were allowed in.

The hospital still had some electricity, thanks to some generators, but it was using its power sparingly, so the hospital's reception was absent of many of the innumerable lights and beeps I'd seen under normal circumstances. The receptionist allowed us up to see Ryan. He looked better than he had when Veronica had hauled him out of the church, not that that was saying much. He gave me a tired smile. "Hey, Sarah."

"Hey. I wanted to check on you. Thought you should know Abby's alright, and Pat's signed up to fight for the Thaleites." I held my hands behind my back, not sure what else to do with them.

Ryan rested back into the pillows. "Cool. Man, I thought hospital food was bad *before* all this." He turned to me. "Is it really the apocalypse?"

"Yeah …"

There was a long silence. Ryan asked, "So, what happens now?"

"A war between heaven and hell, and everyone else fights to survive." My gaze wandered out the window. "Been meaning to ask, did this place have any undead problems when you arrived?"

"Actually, yeah," Ryan said. "Whole bunch of zombies running around the place. Veronica just smashed most of them."

"That'd happen. Barriers between the worlds of living and dead have become unstable; not everyone who dies is going to stay dead. And being undead, uh, tends to drive you crazy."

Ryan nodded. "I'm pretty sure security has that figured out by now. How is Veronica doing?"

A subject I enjoyed. "Haven't heard all that much of her. I get the impression she's been in the field a lot, doing what she does best."

Ryan chuckled. "Don't envy the bad guys. You know, back at the nightclub, I … tried to hit her and she just … *wham.* Bloody hurt, not that I blame her."

"And that was her unarmed and caught off-guard. You saw the kind of kit she was hauling in the church. I once saw her dice an entire horde of demons using nothing but a chainsaw." I smiled, recalling her epic battles.

Ryan nodded again, smiling. "She's probably kicking ass right now."

During the brief lull in conversation, an idea came to me. "Think we could get the roleplaying group up again? With Pat and V. busy, we'd need to find someone else, but I'd like it."

Ryan seemed to think. "I'm … kind of stuck here …"

"We can bring it to you! We all need something to do, right?" I felt a surge of enthusiasm.

Ryan pondered this for a moment. "Sure," he said at last.

Chapter Eight

I had a lot on my mind the next day. For one thing, those of us in the bunker needed to figure out where our next meals were coming from; after no small amount of deliberation, we reluctantly decided to try looting (we *needed* food, the dead didn't). On a brighter note, we also worked on the logistics of getting the roleplaying group back up and running; Abby revealed she'd be happy to run a game, and she was certain she could find another player or two among the refugees at the shelter.

In the evening, Katey came back from scavenging with some food, but she also handed me a letter. "Found this stashed under a rock outside." It was a plain white envelope, with *To Sarah Torren*. It was written in Veronica's handwriting. I quickly tore it open.

Dear Sarah

I might not be able to check on you for a while. I'm about to be deployed on a major op. Can't give you details, of course. I just wanted to write to let you know I'm still thinking of you. Often. It gives me comfort, imagining that one day we might beat back the tide, end the apocalypse, and I'll be able to come home to you. Or maybe just see you again.

I'm still alright. There's a lot of moving around. An asset like me gets thrown into the thick of the fighting. Nothing I can't handle, of course. Coming up against all sorts of things now. Angels, demons, undead, fey—you name it. Doing all sorts of missions, too.

Pat sent word that he's finished his training and has been deployed. Couldn't tell me where. It was nice seeing him in uniform; I have enclosed a photo.

The local Thaleite HQ was hit a few days ago, but since they're going public, you might be able to find a contact with them. If you can, try and send me a letter. It'd be nice to hear you're still alright.

Stay safe for me, puppy.

Veronica

There were two photos in the envelope: one of Pat standing proudly in his new uniform, the other of Veronica in her trusty power armour. I gave the former to Willow, who was delighted, and very carefully stored the letter. Then I set to work writing a reply.

Dear Veronica
Things have been rough, but I'm managing. The bunker's solid and secure, and I don't think anyone else even knows about it. Food's scarce, but we're getting by; the Spire's food stores are still open, even if it is a lot more expensive, so that will keep us going for at least a couple of weeks. Speaking of the Spire, the Circle is in chaos. All the mages running off to join one faction or another. Have you faced any yet? Probably. I'm doing what I can to keep my mind occupied. Abby and Ryan are still alright (apparently Carl makes for one lethal werewombat), and we're working on putting together a new group.
I miss you a lot. I've never felt safer then when you're around, and I dream often of being held in your big, strong arms. But I'd never ask you to stop what you're doing. You're defending all of humanity, and I'm proud of you for that.
Keep giving them hell.
Sarah

Getting the letter posted was easier than I expected; the Spire's postal service was still active, enough to get a message to the Thaleites. Veronica and I started corresponding regularly. Traversing the city—hell, even *surviving*—was still not easy, with the scarcity of food and constant fear of demonic attacks. But the thought of Veronica's next letter was more than enough to motivate me to keep going, scouring the city for my next meal, working through pages and pages of magical theory, and constantly looking for any threat. All of that, just for the chance I might see Veronica again.

One of Veronica's letters read

Attached was a roughly drawn map to the Thaleite's former base in the city, and a diagram of the former barracks layout marking where Veronica's stuff would be. While surviving was taking a lot of effort, retrieving Veronica's stuff would be something productive I could do for my girlfriend, and I had the chance to genuinely help those on the front lines of the war for Earth.

So, the next day, I got Willow and Katey, and we drove to the remains of the Thaleite base, which was hidden beneath an office building downtown. We arrived to find the building in ruins. The gate to the underground carpark had been ripped out.

We slowly picked our way past rubble and wrecked vehicles to what appeared to be the remains of a security checkpoint. All the defences were broken. There were plenty of signs of a fight: bullet holes, spent casings, bloodstains. There was almost nothing of value, likely because either the attackers and/or the Thaleites had picked over the ruins afterwards, taking everything of value. Luckily, that included any of the defences that weren't destroyed in the attack. The only danger we faced was the building's general poor condition, and that wasn't so bad—the Thaleites hadn't skimped when they'd built the place.

Even in its ruined state, the building was an impressive sight. The abandoned technology, while wrecked beyond any use, was clearly bleeding edge, and the base was pretty big for something hidden beneath a city. I wondered if there were any records of it in the city's civic planning.

We managed to get to the barracks without much trouble. What we found there was somewhat discouraging: the entire place had been ransacked. Luckily, whoever had trashed the place had been looking for something more valuable than personal effects, but that still meant the contents of the various lockers was strewn about the barracks under a thin layer of dust. I considered the scene for a moment. "Alright, why don't we collect everything into piles based on where it is? Hopefully that'll make it easier for Veronica and her crew to sort it all out. Then we bundle it all up and take it back to the bunker."

The others agreed, so we got to work. I started with where Veronica's bunk was; I knew her well, so I was pretty confident I'd be able to pick out at least the bulk of her stuff out from the mess. As I worked, I realised that there was no real way of knowing if I was right about that until we'd left.

As I was gathering up some of Veronica's civilian clothes (I identified them by her very pleasant scent), a small piece of paper fell out of one of her pockets. It looked like it had been ripped from a notebook. I picked it up, recognising Veronica's handwriting immediately. Veronica had written me some poetry. I teared up, despite the fact that the poetry was awful—hopefully Veronica would stick to killing demons.

It took an hour or two, but we managed to pile everything into the car and return to the bunker. After we unpacked, I decided to try on Veronica's hoodie. It was so massive on me that I could fit my whole body in the torso without so much as stretching it, which was excellent, since it meant I could surround myself with Veronica's comforting scent. I later sent her a photo of me wearing it.

The wars kept going on the outside. The Spire started to steadily empty out as more and more mages died in the battle for the fate of the world. The city became unpredictable, perfectly safe one day, then bathed in a rain of fire the next. One day, trucks would arrive with enough food to feed an army, the next a water tank would be bombed by cultists.

Throughout it all, we kept living. The roleplaying group got started, and it grew pretty big after some of Ryan's neighbours in the hospital decided they wanted to join in. It even got so big that some splintered off to start their own group. And when that wasn't on, we found other forms of entertainment. With television and the internet crippled, theatre returned to popularity among the survivors, and a local acting troupe managed to make some impressive costumes out of scavenged materials.

One day, I returned from another trip into the Spire to find the bunker door already open. I started readying a wind blast as I slowly entered, fearing disaster. I dismissed the spell when I saw who was standing inside. I lit up in delight. "Veronica!"

My face fell as I saw the scene inside. Willow had fallen to her knees, weeping, and I could hear Katey crying from another room. Veronica's expression was sombre, despite my presence. She simply said, "Pat didn't make it."

I slowly sat on a nearby chair, processing what had happened. The two of us were always on good terms as fellow roleplayers, and we'd become closer friends since the gunfight at the nightclub.

And now he was dead.

"He was on guard duty at a Thaleite outpost when it was hit by angels. Holy fire, straight to the face."

I was silent for a long time. What even was there to say? I couldn't even imagine what Willow or Katey were dealing with. I then felt a surge of resolve. Pat had been counting on his family being safe here, in the bunker. I had made no promises to him, but that wasn't important. If it was the last thing I could do for him, I'd keep his family safe. That's what friends were for, right?

Veronica sat down next to me, wrapping an arm around me. I leaned into her. Then, she scooped me up to hold me closer. I realised that Pat's death was weighing on her as well. We spent a long time like that, embracing each other. Not much was said. Wasn't all that much to say, really. The warmth we got from each other was more than either of us could pack into words.

I tried not to think about how I could thank Pat's death for bringing me a few more moments with the woman I loved.

The day I managed to successfully conjure food, I got cheers from Katey and Willow. The good mood only lasted so long; both were still very much grieving for Pat. I couldn't help but feel powerless. How could I possibly ease the pain of losing a brother and son? Being able to at least mitigate one of the more practical problems eased that frustration, but not completely.

The day after, Veronica returned to the bunker. Willow let her in, and I emerged from the bathroom to find her standing there. Barely. She was covered in bandages and was visibly exhausted. But she was pretending she was just fine. "Hey, puppy."

My eyes bulged. "Veronica! What the hell happened to you!?"

"Got too close to a shoggoth. Relax, it's *much* worse off." She gave her best grin.

I thought about her squadmate, Harry, now killed in action. I remembered it was him I made a promise to, months ago. Time to uphold it. "Honey, you look like you need rest. You get to bed, and I'll make you dinner, okay?"

"Come on, it's not that bad! I feel fine!"

I went for a different approach. "Honey, if you don't get some rest, then it might get worse, and then I'll worry! Get some rest, for me?" I gave her my best puppy-dog eyes.

It worked. Veronica gave a long sigh. "Alright, alright." She walked over to the bed and plopped herself down on it.

She ate the dinner I had made her without complaint, but I could tell she was a little restless, despite everything she had obviously been through. So, after cleaning up, I went to plan B. I nestled onto her chest, careful to lie down in a position that would make it awkward for her to pick me up. I then got comfortable, closed my eyes, and after a moment, started controlling my breathing. As I'd hoped, I heard Veronica mutter something about being stuck.

The war still raged in the outside world. More news came in every day, some good, much bad. One day, I heard of a legion of ghouls breaching a survivor shelter and massacring all inside. Another I heard that the demons had lost a crucial battle against mortal forces. The next I heard that cities were being wiped off the map by angels. Another I heard that Japan had managed to fend off a large-scale angelic attack with some co-ordination between the local kami and some surface-to-air missiles. It was difficult, hearing all these great battles I couldn't actually *do* anything about. I did my best to focus on providing for the few people I could.

Conjuring food took a lot of my time, but I didn't have all that much else to do, so I managed to significantly ease the strain on the bunker's food stores. The food that I could conjure was, unfortunately, incredibly bland, so at Katey's request, I kept up my studies, ducking into the Spire's libraries when I could. I also kept checking the rock that had found itself pressed into service as a post box, and I got another letter from Veronica.

Dear Sarah

The fighting's picking up. Command has a couple of plans going on. One is telling some American oligarchs that hell has oil deposits (does it?); might give the Yanks reason to use all those guns the military-industrial complex has been forcing them to buy.

Good news is I might be seeing you soon. Can't tell you exactly (info security), but turns out command has been talking

*with the Circle, and we've got a major joint op planned. I'll see if
I can get myself an assignment to it; see if you can as well, even if
it's just support.*

*I do want to see you again, even if just for a moment.
You're cute, and you mean a lot to me. And I do really want you to
make one of those extra-large models so I can use it. It would be
awesome; we could have half the other people at the club against
just you and me with those big things. Even the sight of them on
the table alone would be something for pictures.*

Take care of yourself.

Veronica

I got straight to investigating this supposed joint operation
between the Circle and the Thaleites. Unfortunately, I had no
contacts with the Circle's higher echelons, so I couldn't find
much. But as I sat in an empty hall of the Spire, treating myself to
a doughnut enchanted with a crumb-catching charm, I noticed a
summoned task elemental fly past, slapping down some posters
on the wall before flying off to its next destination. I examined the
poster: a call for *all* mages of the Circle to report to a major ritual
spellcasting in a couple of weeks. The last time I'd heard of the
entire Circle being summoned was the early Dark Ages—mainly
because there weren't all that many problems that needed the
sheer power of the whole Circle to solve. Certainly, few were
worth the immense effort of convincing the incredibly fractious
Circle mages to all work together.

I strongly suspected that this was the big plan Veronica
had mentioned (if the Circle's leaders were willing to handle the
labyrinthine politics between the larger supernatural factions,
trying to summon their full power wouldn't have been that much
harder), but I wanted evidence beyond the circumstantial. So, I
headed to the office of my cabal head. The Circle was structured
so that managing academic cabals equated to political power,
meaning their offices were as much centres of political
manoeuvring as they were of magical work. Considering the
effort involved in getting the *entire* Circle in one place, there'd
have to be talk about it there, sooner or later.

It proved to be sooner. I arrived to find an argument already in progress between my boss, Paul and three lower-ranking mages. Paul looked frustrated. "This is from the archmage supreme! Do you think he'd call *everyone* if it wasn't important?"

One of my colleagues, a wart-riddled man who I didn't know by name, growled, "Important for who? He's going to just teleport the whole Spire away!"

A girl even shorter than me with a snappy demeanour that reminded me of a chihuahua took Paul's side. "The Spire's already in another dimension, you idiot!"

"Whatever, Lara! He's just doing it for himself!" the warty man snapped back.

I awkwardly piped up, "Um. Hi!"

Paul sighed. "Sarah. Come to argue too?"

"Um, not yet. Getting more information before taking sides," I said quietly.

"Thank you!" Paul exclaimed. "See, this is how the rest of you should be thinking!"

The fourth mage in the room, a perpetually dishevelled woman whose name I vaguely recalled started with M, spat, "The fucking archmage supreme thinks he can call upon everyone to do whatever he wants!"

Lara's small size seemed to be the only thing stopping her from throwing a punch. "It's the apocalypse! We need major action!"

"Not that kind of action!" M replied.

Lara was halfway through insulting M's personal hygiene when I interrupted. "Hey, hey, hey … okay, can we start with the facts?"

Paul took a deep breath. "Well, the council of archmagi actually agree on something for once. Admittedly, what they've agreed on is something they're even quieter than usual about, but apparently it's a really important plan. So important they say that they can't say anything more in case demons try to stop it."

M detected a chance to spout her conspiracies. "But that would just let the demons know there's something to stop! It's stupid! If there was anything, they'd ——"

Lara wasn't having it. "She asked for *facts!*"

"I'm giving her ——" M started, before I held up a hand to stop her.

"Paul, please continue."

"Not much more to say, actually, other than the fact that there's apparently been meetings between the council and the UN. Anyway, the archmage promises we'll all be told exactly what we're doing on the day."

I chose my next words carefully. "You know, I have heard that a lot of groups are working together on something big. Considering it is the apocalypse …"

The warty man started blathering, "He's just getting rid of his opponents!"

After a few minutes of listening to assorted political commentary and conspiracy theories, I decided my presence wasn't achieving anything, and so I returned to the bunker, where I composed a reply to Veronica.

Dear Veronica

The archmage just ordered a spell be cast by the <u>entire</u> Circle, and I don't envy him trying to get all of us into one place. Apparently, he's co-ordinating with the UN? There's no word on what the spell is, exactly. Apparently it's something demons might try to stop. Could this be the operation you're talking about? Hopefully so. I'll be showing up. On the off chance we get most of the Circle, this could just be enough to end the apocalypse. I'd like to see you home one day.

Don't get me wrong, it's hot how badass you are, saving the world from armies of demons. But when I'm not dreaming about that, I'm dreaming about moving in with you one day. Maybe you could live in the bunker? Or maybe we could buy a new place, a nice flat in the city. I could take care of it while you're gone. If your Thaleite work makes enough money, you could support the both of us, I could keep the place clean, and when you're home … well, I'm sure you can imagine.

Keep fighting, V. This will all end, one day. Something for you to look forward to.

Sarah

The day arrived, and I headed to the Prismatic Spire's test site. The site was in the same extra-dimensional space as the rest of the Spire but separate from the infrastructure of the Spire proper, which allowed for the most dangerous spells to be tested with a measure of safety. In appearance, it was a wide, flat plane of grey dirt-like matter, with rune-inlaid brass arches arcing over it, and beyond that, the nebula-like expanse of the æther. The entire place was abuzz with activity—mages scurrying to and fro and the sentinels doing their best to coordinate everyone.

Shortly after I entered, I presented my identification to the nearby sentinel. "Alright, head over to runic circle 5B and check the runes are up to specification." She handed me a sheet of paper with a series of arcane notes on it.

As I flicked over the specifications, I asked, "So, what exactly *is* it we're doing?"

"Opening a portal into the fortress of the Demon Lord for a strike team on an assassination mission."

Well. That explained a few things. Between the portal having to go between planes of reality, having to penetrate the Demon Lord's immense supernatural defences, and keeping the portal open and active for however long it took to get the strike team in, it made sense that this would require a lot of mages. Maybe not the *entire* Circle, but I doubted all of us were reporting for duty anyway. And it made sense that this was worth it; without a powerful leader to keep them in line, the bulk of the demons would quickly fall into infighting, giving humanity a much better chance at surviving the apocalypse. It also explained why there was a band of soldiers hanging around blasting AC/DC's *Highway To Hell.*

I headed further into the testing ground. As I scanned the area, looking for where I was supposed to be, I did a double take.

There was a damn tank.

A few, actually, and some more armoured vehicles, painted white, "U.N." emblazoned on their hulls. They were to the side, clearly separate from the mages but obviously part of whatever plan the archmage supreme was enacting. A handful of soldiers with blue UN helmets stood here and there, each on edge.

I saw a handful of other supernatural soldiers standing not far from them. A few packs of werekin were scattered around, sitting at various stages on the human–animal spectrum. Some fey creatures were here and there, goblins equipped like parodies of the UN soldiers beside them. A few of the minor gods and their followers had arrived, showing a mix of weapons from the future to the past. The various factions of the world had pooled together some seriously heavy firepower to take on evil incarnate. Which made the absence of The One's followers even more stark.

A sentinel hurriedly asked me to step aside to allow some new arrivals to pass by, and as I did so, I saw some more armoured vehicles approach, these ones painted in dark patchy grey and bearing the insignia of the Thaleites. The sentinels cleared out some space, and the vehicles parked there. A number of soldiers started exiting the vehicles, and I saw at least a dozen wearing power armour.

Veronica was with them. As soon as she saw me, she pulled off her helmet and rushed towards me. "Sarah!" Before I could respond, she scooped me up into her armour-clad arms, kissing me.

I giggled. "It's good to see you. I … I need to get back to work."

Veronica gently set me back down. "Sure, sure. I've been helping set this up for a while."

"By killing demons?"

"And gathering all the demon bits the spell needed," she said. "No idea what you lot use them *for* exactly, but that's not what I get paid to think about. And besides, killing more demons earlier meant not so many for us ——"

We were interrupted by one of the UN soldiers. "Fucking hell, of course you're a dyke."

Veronica's expression shifted to one of barely contained rage. She slowly turned to face the soldier, an older man with pepper-black facial hair and a sneer. Veronica clenched her fists. "The *fuck* are you doing here?"

"Following orders," he said, placing heavy emphasis on every syllable.

Veronica bared her teeth. "You should be in fucking jail."

The man snapped back, "I should have shot you for treason!"

Veronica took a step towards him. "How many innocent people are dead because of you?"

"Innocent?" The man scowled. "Those people were scum."

When Veronica's hand drifted towards her weapon, I wrapped my arms around hers. "Honey, maybe we should leave this until *after* we kill the incarnation of all evil?" At the conflicted and frustrated look Veronica gave me, I elaborated, "Look, I'm all for shooting war criminals. Just … I think he's a little lower on the list than the actual Demon Lord, don't you think?"

Veronica sighed, and relaxed, just a bit. I released her arm. She turned and headed towards where the Thaleites were mustering, glaring at the soldier as she did so. The feeling was apparently mutual, as the soldier glared back at her, then at me, before returning to his men.

One of the other Thaleite soldiers, also clad in power armour, had observed the exchange. "*You're* the commander's girlfriend?"

"She's a commander? Veronica?" I already knew she was badass, but I hadn't realised she was a high-ranking badass.

"Promoted pretty recently, but she's good at this. Lot worse people I could be following into hell. Literally. Piece of work, ain't she?" The Thaleite looked over to where Veronica was checking her weapons.

I smiled widely. "Yeah, she is. Have you heard about the time that she beat the crap out of a cop?"

"Along with the rest of the company. Honestly, half of us are jealous of you. Other half are scared she'll crush our skulls." The Thaleite paused for a second. "Actually, there's a pretty big overlap there."

I giggled. "She did break my jaw once. Totally worth it."

The Thaleite laughed. "How the hell did you net *her*?"

"By being a massive dork, apparently."

"Figures. Anyway, I better let you get back to work. This spell looks pretty big." The Thaleite gave me a nod before returning to his unit.

I wasn't sure how much time passed; the tension of what was happening stretched out every second. But eventually, the Archmagi gave the signal to cast the spell. The ætheric sky above us thrummed as we pulled the mana from it and shaped it. It bounced and echoed between us in carefully constructed patterns, and over the course of nearly an hour, the spell began to take shape. Finally, a rift between realities began to form. Space rippled and warmed into a whirlpool, and in its centre …

Light.

Bright, blinding light, and behind it, the heavens.

We were facing The One.

The strike team hesitated; this wasn't where they were expecting the portal to open to. Everyone looked to their superiors, most of whom didn't have any better ideas than their subordinates. I expected most believed the spell had misfired; I certainly did.

Then, there was a voice—quiet, and yet it came from everywhere.

The corrupt defile heaven again.

Uh-oh.

Chapter Nine

There was a blinding flash of light as a wave of holy fire descended on the testing ground. The ground shook as the archmagi cast a counterspell, and the entire dimension trembled under the weight of the world's greatest wizards striving against the will of The One.

Then came the angels, descending like apocalyptic meteors. The battle escalated as the strike team opened fire on the angels. The mages fell into disarray, some fleeing, some fighting. I ducked, pumping all the mana I could gather into my wards. I felt a surge of panic and found my mind reaching for any skerrick of reassurance.

Veronica.

In my panic, I hadn't considered that she had other things to worry about. Seeking safety, I rushed towards where the Thaleites had been deployed. As I ran, the voice of the archmage supreme echoed across the field. "Mages! Close the portal, now!" In theory, it wasn't all that hard. The portal would only exist as long as there was a spell to sustain it, and the spell would only exist as long as there was both mana to fuel it and a runic construct to support it. Draining the mana and collapsing the construct was straightforward, even with the complete disarray of the mages assembled—after all, we were the ones who had cast the spell in the first place. The spell construct fizzled out quickly.

But the portal remained open. The One simply established a whole new construct in its place. While it resembled a spell, its construction was noticeably different, and vastly more difficult to dispel, especially since it wasn't *our* spell construct. Angels kept pouring through the portal, and The One continued to channel its wrath. The only reason we hadn't already been obliterated against the sheer power of The One is that the archmagi, for all their disagreements, managed to agree that they didn't want to be killed, and they had turned their immense power towards fending off The One. But there was only so much they could do; support from the rest of the Circle was intermittent and poorly coordinated, and the strike team could only do so much against the hordes of angels.

I reached the Thaleites. Their guns were focused on the air, cutting down swathes of angels as yet more took their place. I found the nearest armoured vehicle and ducked into its shadow, hoping it would give me some kind of shelter. I paid for my safety with the deafening noise of a hundred guns firing into the sky, my ears ringing with their rapport. I covered my ears, trying in vain to block out the thunder.

Veronica noticed me, hurrying to my side even as she fired volleys into the sky. "Grab onto my back!" She didn't have time to say any more, simply crouching down as she gave orders to some of her comrades. I nearly leapt onto her back, wrapping my arms around her neck and finding footholds in her ammo pouches. Veronica stood, and I clung to her like she was holding me above a deadly drop. She gave no sign that this was any problem and simply resumed the battle.

My danger ring thrummed, and I pumped my wards with mana as a blast of holy fire clipped Veronica in the side. It struck me as well. Even through the wards, I felt a scalding pain. Veronica's armour seemed to have taken the worst of the hit, but I noticed her stagger just slightly. Suddenly, I realised I *could* do something to help; my conjuration magic would provide some cover to the Thaleites. Not much, but it was *something*, and honestly, being able to do anything at all reassured me, regardless of how much it actually helped. Casting spells isn't easy when you have tinnitus and you need most of your limbs to cling on to your super-soldier girlfriend for dear life, but I managed to command just enough mana to deflect a blast or two.

Veronica paused now and then to bark orders and reports into a radio. I was focused on the raining death, so I didn't catch what was being said until Veronica finally got my attention. "Sarah!"

I had to yell to hear myself over the gunfire. "Yeah?"

"Can you find us a portal out of here?" Her tone made it sound like she was repeating herself.

I wasn't overly familiar with the areas of the Spire nearest the testing ground, but after thinking a moment, I realised I could plot a route to a portal back to Earth. A portal large enough to fit the Thaleite vehicles was a more complicated problem, but I could think of one that was *probably* large enough. "Um, I think so!"

Veronica wasn't in the mood for doubt. She paused a moment, then spoke into her radio. "I've got a mage here that can plot us a route. Taking her to you." She then rushed across the battlefield, her armour's powered exoskeleton propelling us with impressive speed. She ducked behind another armoured vehicle, where an athletic older man, evidently the commander of the Thaleite detachment, was barking orders into a radio. She turned her back to him and crouched down. It took a moment for me to muster the will to disengage from the safety I felt from Veronica, but I managed it. I ducked into the vehicle's shadow.

The commander looked at me. "You got a route?"

"I think so," I stammered.

The commander was evidently not happy with my uncertainty. He showed none himself. "Fucking—dammit, best option." He grabbed me by the shoulder and pulled me inside the vehicle. He then addressed the driver, "On my order, take point. We're getting out of here. She'll direct you to our portal out."

I gulped. I was suddenly under a lot of pressure. The driver, a stocky Asian woman, looked at me expectantly. I tried my best to break the route down into steps. Navigation was pretty difficult from the confines of the armoured vehicle, which was built more for the protection of the crew and passengers than actually looking around. Still, I managed something. "Um, alright … do a U-turn, then head to … hold on …" I quickly doubled back to a nearby hatch, climbing up to peer out from the roof. I returned to the driver. "Third arch from the left; that's where we're going."

The Thaleite soldiers headed back to their armoured vehicles, still fighting off the legions of angels. The transport got a lot more cramped, and I tried not to think about how many of the vehicle's occupants were seriously wounded. The commander gave an order and the Thaleite vehicles fell into formation, heading back into the Spire. It occurred to me that I'd only ever traversed the Spire on foot; guiding an entire armoured convoy through would be an entirely different problem.

But I managed it. It took a combination of good spatial awareness, improvisation, sheer damn luck, and taking advantage of the fact that the Thaleite vehicles could go straight through some walls, but I managed to get the convoy to the portal in question. It had been established by the Circle specifically for larger amounts of cargo, placed between a few warehouses. But while it was large, whether or not it was larger than the vehicles we were about to drive through it was a solid 50/50. The vehicle's driver looked at it with a frown. "This it?"

"Yeah. Look, I only had a few seconds; it was the best I could think of."

The driver seemed to consider the problem a while. Then, the entire Spire shook. Behind us, the Spire itself warped, cracked, fragmented and fell away. The One was tearing it to pieces. The commander's eyes bulged. "Fuck it! Dismount the turrets, retract the antennas, then pedal to the metal!"

No-one was in a position to object, so a moment later, the convoy rushed through the portal. It was a tight fit, and one or two of the vehicles lost their roofs, but everyone made it out. The convoy found itself in a hilly region, with some train tracks to the side. As the convoy regrouped, the commander asked me, "Alright, where are we?"

"Good question! Earth, definitely. I'm pretty sure this is an hour or two out from Sydney."

The commander sighed then turned to a nearby navigator, instructing them to get a GPS connection. Meanwhile, the convoy came to a stop, and the commander called a meeting with the team's other leaders. I slowly followed him out of the vehicle. From another transport came Veronica. A massive hole was rent in her armour, and beneath that I could see burnt flesh. She barely seemed to notice, removing her helmet and giving me a wide smile. "There! All good!"

The commander frowned. "Not exactly the best plan there, Wainwright."

This dampened Veronica's mood. "I didn't see you come up with a better one!"

The commander shook his head. "I'll get us a new route. For now, talk to a medic."

Veronica rolled her eyes. "It's fine, the armour took the
_____"

"Veronica!" I snapped. "You are going to sit down and do as little as possible until the medic has had a look at you."

There was a pause. Veronica looked like she was about to argue but then sat down with a huff. I approached her. "Alright, now let me help you out of all that armour to make the medic's job easier."

Veronica raised an eyebrow. "Didn't you find it sexy?"

"I'm kind of busy being concerned with your burns. Once the medic gives the all-clear, *then* I'll fawn dramatically over your epic battle scars."

It was as I was telling her this that another of Veronica's squad approached, this one marked as a medic. As I helped remove Veronica's armour and let the medic do their work, I realised that the rest of the Thaleites were giving me looks—some surprised, some impressed, some amused, most a combination of the three. Eventually, the medic finished working. Her voice was surprisingly high-pitched for a large woman in power armour. "Alright, that'll keep it from getting worse, but you need to talk to medical."

Veronica was halfway through moaning an objection when I interrupted, "No arguing with the medic!"

Veronica fell silent. One of her squadmates jabbed, "Holy shit, it's the Veronica whisperer."

Meanwhile, the portal to the Spire shuddered and closed. I looked back at it with a wince before turning to the Thaleite commander. "Hey, uh, could you arrange a ride back home for me?"

As the commander considered the matter, Veronica said, "Look, she's my girlfriend, and she helped us out. Hell, I'll carry her back home myself if I have to."

This seemed to give the commander an idea. He addressed the medic. "Is Wainwright up to driving?"

"Nothing intense, and I'd say she needs rest straight afterwards, but it wouldn't make things worse, sir."

The commander nodded. "Alright, we head back to the nearest base for medical attention, Wainwright can take the mage home from there." He addressed Veronica, "But I want you to co-operate with the doctors, understood?"

Veronica was audibly not happy. "Yes, sir."

Soon enough, Veronica and I were driving a scavenged car down the empty highway. The fight had taken a lot out of the both of us, and the ride was mostly silent. Too exhausted to remain alert, my mind simply wandered through the events of the past few hours, days and months. I wondered at length why the spell had opened a portal straight to The One, rather than the Demon Lord. When I came up with nothing, I then pondered why The One and their followers were so consistently hostile, clearly more focused on fighting humans then demons.

Then I realised those problems might be connected.

"Veronica?"

"Yeah, puppy?"

"Do you think—okay, I can't prove this or anything, it's really just speculation—but … could The One … *be* the Demon Lord?"

Veronica gripped the steering wheel tighter. "Fuck …"

I shook my head. "Look, it's just a thought, but I was wondering why the spell opened a portal there, and ——"

"And the angels have been giving people more trouble than demons. Runs against the entire point of the apocalypse," Veronica finished for me. "Maybe it's been like this the whole time. Ryan, the Templars, the angels …"

I analysed the problem, extrapolating its consequences. "I'd talk to my higher-ups about it, but with what happened to the Spire, I don't know how many of them are left. Surely some of them had to have escaped. When we get back, I'll see if I can talk to any of the other mages. One of them will have to have a better idea of what happened."

"Sounds like a plan. I'll suggest this to my superiors; we've got some pretty sharp knives working for us." The weight of what we were discussing wasn't lost on either of us, but we were simply too exhausted to panic.

After a while longer driving, I had another idea. "What about fallen angels?"

"What about them?"

"Remember a couple of months before the apocalypse, when Ryan was saved from some angels by a group of fallen?" I'd told her all about the incident before.

"Yeah. I mean, we don't *know* there was more than one fallen angel, but I've seen groups of fallen angels since. Never stuck around to talk; not that anyone really trusts them anyway. But you're thinking they know something?"

I leaned back in my seat. "They would, if we're right. Also, this all started because Ryan was looking into fallen angels. Well, I think that's why. That's what he was doing when the Templars nabbed him. I think that first angel you took out took offence to me helping him."

Veronica drummed her fingers on the steering wheel. "But how do we talk to them? The fallen angels, I mean?"

"Good question."

I spent next part of the drive trying to find a solution to that problem and not coming up with much. An hour later, I had another question. "That UN soldier you were yelling at …"

"He was my CO. He ordered …" Veronica trailed off. I knew exactly what she was talking about.

It was midnight by the time we made it to the bunker. A moment after I opened the door, I was greeted by Willow and Katey, the noise of the door opening evidently having woken them up. When they saw me, their expressions turned from panic to relief. Willow cried, "Sarah! Where have you been?"

"The spell we were casting went wrong," I replied wearily. "Short version is, God blew up the Spire, Veronica and I barely got out. Long version can wait until we've got some sleep."

Willow and Katey were perfectly understanding, so Veronica plopped herself down on my bed, and I plopped myself down on top of her. We were both too exhausted to even move. Still, it gave me that contact with her I had dearly missed.

I woke up much later than usual for obvious reasons, but still a bit before Veronica. A good night's sleep somewhere safe did wonders for me. I assumed it would also be good for

Veronica, but her condition had been much worse to start off with. I spent a while lying there. Not so much out of exhaustion or comfort (in fact, my stomach was sending me a reminder that I hadn't eaten for a while), but to indulge in Veronica's presence that little bit longer. Her heat, her scent, her touch, the way her chest slowly rose and fell.

Eventually, my need for food overpowered my need for affection, and I crept out of the bedroom and got something to eat. When I finished, Veronica still hadn't woken. I slowly crept back to her side and gently ran my hand across her, feeling her breath, the beating of her heart, the curve of her muscles. I was a little concerned that something was wrong, but I was no doctor. But that thought led to another: Veronica had a reputation for pushing herself hard, doctor's orders be damned. Maybe her body was just catching up on all that sleep her wrath had denied it? If so, her rest wasn't to be disturbed. I carefully wrapped her in a blanket. I kissed her on the forehead, then headed to my lab to conjure more food.

It was nearly midday by the time Veronica finally awoke. She slowly walked into the lab. I could see how her shoulders sagged under the weight of so many brutal battles. "Morning!"

Veronica scoffed. "Barely. Sorry for sleeping in on you."

"What? Honey, if I had a problem, I would have woken you. Hell, after all you've been through, you needed your sleep."

Veronica frowned. "The demon hordes don't sleep."

"Yes, they do."

"Not what I meant. Individuals, some time, but there'll always be another, doing what they do. Someone's got to fight them." Just beneath Veronica's words, I could hear an intense, fundamental hatred, the kind of hatred that made words like 'loathe' and 'scorn' necessary.

I tried to calm her. "Well, that's what the US army's doing, right? That ludicrous number of guns—the demons are probably learning why the US doesn't have healthcare."

Veronica softly chuckled. "Sure. Anyway, you get a chance to talk to other mages yet?"

"Not yet. I was going to head to the shelter at lunchtime, see if anyone else escaped." The subject reminded me I had a spell to work on, and I got to doing some arcane arithmetic.

"Alright. I'll talk to my people, see if any of them know anything about it. Maybe they can find other surviving mages. If we're right …" She sighed.

I was still a little worried about her and decided I'd rather she stay, perhaps a bit selfishly. "Alright. But, if you're still available, it's been a while since we've been able to play any games together. What do you think?"

"I'd like that."

So that's how I ended up nerding out about fictional space tanks with a woman that had fought angels not a day before. The contrast wasn't really something that occurred to me often. Veronica Wainwright was one of the most lethal soldiers on the planet, and she was also a bit of a nerd. There wasn't any contradiction in that. One lead into the other once in a while, like the time I first fell for her…

***

A year earlier

The games store was surprisingly quiet during the day, which made it an excellent place for some sensory reprieve in a welcoming environment after a long day of shopping. I arrived to find Veronica standing by the racks of paints, examining a list contemplatively. I walked up beside her. "Hey."

She glanced at me briefly. "Hey."

I glanced at the list. "Something up?"

Veronica crinkled the list in frustration. "The paints I want aren't in stock, and the next lot aren't in for a month. All that money …"

"Actually, you don't need the official paints. Friend of mine worked out there's this one paint set you can get in department stores, sticks to the plastic just like the official stuff, and you can get a whole palette for the price of a single pot."

Veronica glanced at the tiny pots and their not-so-tiny price tags. "Know which?"

I dug around for the name, only to find that my brain had discarded it in order to make room for expansions in the fanfiction department. "Uh, I forget." An idea. "I could show it to you—the department store across the street should have a set."

Veronica smiled. "Sure, thanks."

A short walk later, I was browsing the aisles at the nearby department store. I'd just found what we were looking for when we overheard some shouting from the clothing section. "What are you doing, traitor? Are you just throwing out centuries of work?"

Veronica clearly wasn't one to stand by when there was conflict, and she strode over to investigate. I quickly grabbed the paints before following her. We turned some shelves to find two women—one an older woman with pepper-brown hair and a figure that showed she didn't mind a few serves of cake. She was yelling at a cowering second woman, much younger, barely out of teenage years, and an obvious tomboy, with cropped hair. The argument also seemed to be happening in the men's section. The older woman shouted, "You're a disgrace! You think they care about us!? You're scum!"

Veronica approached with folded arms, cutting a calm yet imposing figure. "Is there a problem?"

The older woman seemed galvanised at the prospect of reinforcements. "This bitch thinks she can be a man!"

I looked closer at where the other person was shying away, seeing a pin labelled 'he/him'. I corrected my 'tomboy' assumption, though the man was clearly transgender and very early in his transition. Veronica simply looked at him and politely asked, "Excuse me, can I ask your gender?"

The man awkwardly stammered, "I- I'm a man."

Veronica turned to the woman, fire in her eyes. "Apologise to the man."

She seemed genuinely shocked that her 'righteous feminism' wasn't all that popular. "W-what!? Don't you ——"

Veronica wasn't about to entertain this. She grabbed the front of the other woman's shirt, looming over her, and her voice turned dangerously low, holding a tone that set my heart racing. *"Apologise."*

The woman gulped. "Um … s-sorry."

Veronica wasn't finished. "And you will address him as 'sir'. Now, do it properly!"

"S-sorry, s-sir," she stuttered, clearly unused to being seriously threatened.

Veronica released her. "Right, now if you so much as litter, you damn well better hope it's security that catches you, not me. Now beat it!" As the woman scurried off, Veronica relaxed, her expression turning friendly and helpful. "You alright, mister?"

The man clearly hadn't been referred to as such before, and he was obviously enjoying it. "Um, yeah. Thanks."

I watched Veronica effortlessly stand down from her fight-ready stance, happily offering to stand guard while the man did some shopping to further masculinise his wardrobe, as if playing hero was just another day for her. I wasn't really paying all that much attention; I was too busy falling head-over-heels in love.

***

The present

I arrived at the shelter a bit after lunch. I was wearing my Circle amulet openly, hoping to catch the attention of another Circle mage. After scanning the crowd a while, I found one my colleagues. She had a haunted look about her; not that that was remotely unusual these days. I walked up to her. "Harriet! Glad to see you're alright."

She half-laughed in relief. "Sarah! Were you there for the major spell?"

I couldn't process, let alone express, the sheer gravity of all that was happening, so I didn't try. Instead, I kept my speech deceptively calm. "The one that opened a portal straight to The One? Yeah. Seen anyone else from the Circle around?"

Harriet shook her head. "No, I …" She paused, visibly blinking back tears. "The Spire's gone. The One tore it apart."

I decided to get to the point. "You know, I was wondering why the portal didn't open to the Demon Lord … and I think … maybe it did."

Harriet's eyes slowly widened. "Bullshit."

"Look, it's really just speculation at this point, but there's been a whole lot of strange things happening with The One, angels and churches for years, right? And my girlfriend's a Thaleite, and she says she's been running into *groups* of fallen angels," I explained. "So, I was thinking, if The One *is* the Demon Lord, the fallen angels would have to know, right?"

"Do you have a plan?"

"Er, that's where I hit a roadblock. I was wondering if you had any ideas," I said awkwardly.

Harriet leaned heavily on a nearby table, as if she didn't have enough hope or energy to support herself. "No … I mean, I know my friend Kavita had done a lot of research into them, but … she didn't make it."

I was never the best at sympathy. "Oh, I'm sorry. Did she keep any notes?"

"In the Spire."

A dead end. My shoulder's slumped. "Oh … well, thanks anyway."

Veronica's power armour was bulky enough to make it impractical for times where she wasn't expecting a fight, and its power requirements were substantial, so she had left it to charge while she went to talk to the local Thaleites. Since I got back to the bunker before her, that gave me time enough to get a closer look. The battle damage it had incurred gave me a solid look at its inner workings. That look only amounted to so much, as the engineering was very sophisticated—far beyond my rudimentary understanding. I did notice a slight magic-disruptive weave throughout the armour, lead I suspected, though it would be an engineering nightmare compensating for the metal's weight and conductivity.

But the weave was beneath the armour plates; enough to afford the wearer a measure of protection against magic. The armour plates themselves could be affected by magic normally.

So, I decided to give Veronica a little present, one that would improve her chances at coming back home to me.

My efforts nearly got me blown up a couple of times; the armour plates were made out of some kind of unfamiliar alloy, and it took me a while to figure out how magic interacted with it. It also took some finesse to avoid interfering with the armour's electronics and motors. But I managed to paint on some runes that would improve the armour's resilience.

Veronica returned as I was working. She it looked over with a frown. "Hey, puppy … what are you doing?"

"Nothing major, just one or two structural integrity runes. Small ones. Didn't want to interfere with anything important, but I wanted to do something to help." I gave her a hopeful look.

She picked up one of the armour pieces, examining what I'd done. "Hm … alright then. How much longer is it going to take?"

"About …" Not a question that was ever easy to answer, but I managed to pull out a number, "… another hour or two."

"Cool. After that, I'll give it a test run, make sure you haven't broken anything." She set the armour back on the table.

I pondered reminding her to take it easy for the next day or two, but I decided that I'd need to do so just before she set off anyway, so I left the matter for now. I opted instead to change the subject. "Did you turn up anything about fallen angels?"

"One or two things, actually. Not sure how much I'm at liberty to tell you, but they seem to have made angels their priority targets, and they aren't shy about shooting The One's other followers. As to how to talk to them, no luck so far. You?"

"Nothing. Without the Spire's libraries …" I sighed, setting down my work and burying my head in my hands.

Veronica cooed, "Hey, hey, come here." She gently picked me up in the bridal carry I *very much* enjoyed. I nestled in closer to her. She whispered, "We'll be alright. I'll kill every damn demon if I have to."

I mumbled, "We've lost so much … and we're lucky!"

"This will all end, Sarah. I'll end it myself. I promise."

Chapter Ten

The next day, after confirming my work hadn't inadvertently damaged the power armour, Veronica left to resume her fight. She said she felt a lot better going into battle wearing my work. It was somewhat reassuring, but I would miss her, nevertheless. In order to keep my mind busy, I continued working at the problem of how I could prove, or disprove, that The One and the Demon Lord were one and the same.

I checked all the nearby portals to the Spire, and all had either vanished or turned dangerously unstable. One or two had some fragments of the Spire littered around them. One was rapidly switching destinations between dozens of different planes, a dozen times a second; another was warping space and time around it. It didn't surprise me terribly.

With the Spire pretty much ruled out, I didn't have many avenues when it came to research. So, I kept up with the avenue of tracking down some fallen angels. I couldn't do that directly, but I hoped that I could track them by locating their enemies. Figuring out what The One's followers were doing wasn't exactly easy, but it was very much doable. The local authorities regularly updated the survivors on the general activities of the various factions now fighting over the Earth, and that included information about several nearby towns and villages that had been taken over by various churches. I then had to try and predict where the fallen would strike. If Ryan's rescue was any indication, the fallen would seek to save survivors from The One's followers. However, figuring out where they'd intervene would require knowing where The One was about to make a move, and that was a tricky prospect.

Veronica and the Thaleites didn't turn up much, at least not that Veronica was able to tell me. Apparently the demons had thrown everything they had at Thaleite HQ and killed a significant number of Thaleite diplomatic and intelligence personnel (though Veronica assured me that, strategically, the damage was far from crippling, and the attack had cost the demons dearly).

Meanwhile, I had an idea regarding a more practical subject: I had got pretty good at making basic protective charms, and they were in very high demand. So, I made some and traded them to survivors for other supplies. Katey turned out to be a big help; while she wasn't magically inclined, she had a knack for arts and crafts, so she focused on constructing all the physical parts of the charms, allowing me to focus on the magic.

On one trip to the shelter, I saw an optimistic bulletin: The One's followers had been driven from the city. If the war kept going well, people in the city could eventually return to some sense of normalcy. It was as I was leaving the shelter from that trip that something occurred to me: the Templars had a base under a church—the one where all this arguably started, the one that Veronica had trashed. The Vatican controlled information pretty carefully, but there were definitely holy relics there last I checked. How much would be left after all this time, and all this chaos, was a mystery, but if The One's followers really had been driven from the city, then there couldn't be all that much harm in me checking.

I wasn't an idiot. I knew the city could still be very dangerous, and there might still be security systems or defensive wards around the church, so I was careful to prepare. I spent the next night and morning reviewing various defensive and illusion magics and made sure my pouch of magical reagents was fully stocked. Willow wanted to come along, and I seriously considered it, but my magics were barely enough to cover myself; if there was trouble, I couldn't protect her. I wasn't Veronica, after all. But it was safe enough for her to drive me to the church, so that's what we did.

'Eerily quiet' was could be used in describing many places after the apocalypse, but that meant a new term would be needed for the emptiness of the church, and how every little sound I made swelled to fill the entire soundscape, like the tinkling as my foot brushed some bullet cartridges that littered the ground. Someone had been in the church to remove the bodies of the Templars Veronica had taken out (sanctification would probably prevent them from getting up and walking off themselves, even with the barriers between the living and dead not being what they used to be), but little else had changed. I could still see where

Veronica had blown her way through the wall, and a crater or two where she'd fired her grenade launcher.

I slowly advanced through the church, retracing the steps we had taken to the underground level. I advanced slowly, carefully trying to identify what few sounds echoed in the distance; the creak of my foot against the floorboards and the groaning of a beam. But nothing happened as I made my way down.

I looked around at the underground chamber where Veronica had fought the angel. Pretty much everything had been removed, and it almost looked like a wholly different room. But the cell was still there, and still with a bent-open bar. I could also see some scattered bloodstains and a single dropped pistol. I examined the latter for a while. Veronica had taught me one or two things about guns just before the apocalypse, and her first lesson had been that they were *very* dangerous. I wasn't a monster hunter, but in the age of the apocalypse …

Hands trembling, I slowly picked it up, careful to keep my hands away from the trigger. The first thing I did was look for the safety catch. I found it eventually and noted it was in the 'safe' position. Out of anxiety (or, for something so dangerous, wisdom), I carefully pointed it away from myself and at a blank spot on the far wall, and then I pulled the trigger. *Click*. Sighing in relief, I stuffed it in my handbag, lacking a proper holster.

I then got back to what I was doing. Finding that the basement was otherwise empty, I returned to the ground level. Looking throughout the church, I found what appeared to be a library. It hadn't been caught in the crossfire of the fight a few months ago. Apparently, its occupants had left in a hurry; there were still books open on tables, and an unfinished note in a nearby log.

I was about to start scouring the shelves for lore when I noticed a strange tear in the nearby wallpaper; one that ran straight up and down. With a frown, I approached it. Gently running my finger across it, I felt a gap in the wall. I gently knocked, and part of the wall gave ever so slightly. I'd found a secret door! Pressing on it, I noticed it had a bit more give towards the top, which led me to conclude that whatever mechanism was keeping it shut was towards the bottom. A quick search led me to that mechanism: the skirting board beneath the door was loose, and removing it revealed a small keyhole. I hadn't the faintest idea where the key was, and the odds of it having been spirited away from the city was too great for me to spend much time looking for it.

So, I turned to thinking of ways to force the door open. Luckily, I'd done a major research project on the conjuration of sharp objects. So, over the course of about a minute, I planned a spell to conjure a wedge. Then, I realised that if I wanted to force the door open, it would be much simpler to just bash it open with something solid, like my new gun. It took a few strikes, and experimenting with striking the door in different places. Fortunately, the months hadn't been kind to either lock or door, and both already relied more on secrecy than sturdiness.

Then I heard the sound of a number of engines approaching. I tensed further. If I was lucky, it could just be a patrol of the local Thaleites or authorities. If I wasn't lucky … I needed to leave, quickly. But the promises of a secret door were just too tempting. Two more strikes, and the lock popped off.

I opened the door to see a circle, heavily sanctified and magically isolated, just enough for a small table and one occupant. On the table was an orb, set within a series of rings, each enclosed within the other so that none could be released but each could spin freely. Each one was inscribed with symbols. When I stepped within the circle, I could feel intense magic flowing through it. I had no doubt it was a powerful artefact, but learning more would have to wait.

I glanced out of the window and caught a faint glimpse of a red cross, either medics or the Templars. Moments later, a few of them passed by the window, confirming it was the latter. It was time to leave. I shoved the artefact into my bag and turned to leave—only to discover that the hallway out contained a back entrance, and I could see figures moving from beyond the stained-glass windows. I gulped and ducked back into the library. Heart pounding like a drum, I searched for a hiding place.

The secret door.

Now I'd broken it open, it was a bit more obvious, but I wasn't swimming in options, and the magical isolation would also safeguard me from most magical forms of divination, which could save my life if the Templars had an angel with them. I ducked inside, pulling the door shut as best I could (without a handle on the interior, I was forced to leave it slightly ajar), and ducked behind the table. For once, I was thankful that my body had really just considered puberty to be a suggestion; I was small enough to fit into *very* tight spaces.

A second later, I heard the library door open. I heard a soldier call *clear*, followed by a dozen footsteps. I cast a simple illusion spell to hide myself. It was hard without incantations, but I'd been studying a spell for just this situation, and in the darkness of the secret compartment, I didn't need anything complicated, just enough to make it no longer obvious where I was.

I finished the casting with barely a millisecond to spare. A Templar opened up the passage. He didn't even look at me, clearly focused on the table that I'd left empty. "It's gone!"

Another Templar appeared behind him. "What!? *Fuck!*"

The Templar crouched quickly, looking underneath the table. I focused every iota of my strained will towards keeping my illusion up. My heart raced.

The Templar stood, turning away. "Alright, sweep the rest of the church, look for any scavs. They might have left a trail." I was straining my mind like an exhausted muscle as the Templars turned and left. Just as they turned away, my grip on the spell slipped. Fortunately, they didn't notice.

I had to stop myself from sighing in relief; that had already been *far* too close for comfort, but the Templars would be in the church for a while yet. It was too dangerous for me to leave, but I was willing to gamble they wouldn't bother checking the secret compartment again, so I could simply wait until they left. It was far from comfortable (my bladder was beginning to make itself known), but it was far better than running the risk of being shot. For now, I kept myself occupied by drawing some runes on the ground that would allow me to sustain an illusion for longer, in case a Templar decided to double-check.

It was as I was doing so that something more worrying occurred to me: Willow was still out there, parked nearby. The Templars wouldn't have to sweep all that far to find her. But what I could do? Taking on the Templars was simply out of the question (Veronica was a decent teacher, but I was still nowhere near good enough to handle even a single soldier, let alone a whole squad). Escape was *possible*, but I'd have to reach her without being detected. I wasn't so good at illusion to move with any real speed while maintaining one.

I wrestled with the problem for a solid minute. Finally, guilt overpowered my fear: I *couldn't* just leave Willow out there, at the Templars' mercy. Taking a deep breath, I slowly crept out, watching where I put my feet, careful to not make a sound. My ears strained to keep track of the dozen or so pairs of boots as they moved. If the Templars caught a whiff of me, I was dead. I heard them move in a practised pattern, carefully spreading out from the rear of the church. I realised that they'd assumed they hadn't missed anything. So, I slowly crept to the same door they had come in. I opened it ever so slightly and peered through.

I saw them dragging Willow into a van.

My heart plummeted into the abyss. They were taking her alive, but after what had happened to Ryan, that wasn't much comfort. But what could I do? I wasn't a battlemage. I couldn't barter with them; even with the artefact, they had no reason not to kill me and take what they wanted. There was a lot I could make, but all that took time, and I had a minute at most.

I had to face facts: there wasn't a damn thing I could do. Save for watching, powerless, as the van drove away.

The city's public transport had, prior to the apocalypse, been so good that I never needed to learn to drive. With Willow gone, her car was useless to me. Without transport, I had no choice but to walk back home. My every step was weighed down by guilt, like lead around my ankles. Pat had counted on his family being safe in the bunker, and now? Death wasn't even the worst thing that could happen to Willow. She could have been safe, but I *had* to start poking my nose where it didn't belong. What was I even thinking? I wasn't Veronica. Hell, *Pat* had more right to call himself a hero, sacrificing himself for humanity. And how did I honour that sacrifice? By getting his mother captured. Thoughts of self-punishment swam through my mind. How could I possibly make amends for what I'd done? How would I explain it to Katey?

I was too exhausted, physically and emotionally, to keep my guard up. Which is why I was startled to hear a woman's voice. "Excuse me." I yelped, jumping back and reaching for my reagent pouch. I saw the woman: the woman that had saved Ryan from angels, the possible fallen angel, the same dog at her side. She looked apologetic. "Sorry for startling you. I just noticed you have a magical artefact."

I clutched what I'd taken from the church. "What's it to you?"

Her tone was gentle and instructive. "Simply put, I know what it is and how it works. It's awfully dangerous; it could get you in serious trouble."

"Let me guess: you want it."

"In so many words," she said. "But I'll pay you for it."

An idea. "Templars just kidnapped a friend of mine. Willow is her name. Took her from the church, some blocks up that way." I pointed in the direction I'd come from. "You bring her back to the shelter in one piece, the artefact's all yours."

The woman seemed to be considering the idea. "Can I ask what she was doing in the church?"

"Well, she wasn't in the church, exactly; she was waiting outside to pick me up. I went into the church, looking for information on fallen angels." I fixed her with a look. "I think I may have had some success."

The woman raised an eyebrow. "Have you?"

I took a deep breath. "A few weeks ago, the whole Spire made a plan to open a portal to the Demon Lord so a strike team could take him out. It opened a portal to The One. I was thinking … are they one and the same?"

The woman nodded, slowly and gravely.

I had already pondered the terrible implications of this, so all that was left to feel was … gratification. I half-laughed. "Fuck.

That's … wow. I … I take it that's why so many of you angels are falling, right? Because you *are* a fallen angel, right?"

"Yeah. The dog, too." The dog punctuated her words with a quick wag of the tail.

"Can I pet him?"

The woman laughed as the dog trotted up to me. After the awful events of the day, some canine comfort was sorely needed. I gave the dog some thorough scratches and belly rubs, enjoying the feeling of the soft fur under my fingers. The dog, even being a fallen angel, seemed to enjoy the attention.

Meanwhile, the humanoid angel explained, "It happened some decades ago, by your calendar. Couldn't say *exactly* when, but I think it was a bit before the War of Three Truths. The Demon Lord managed to sneak *into* The One and take control. He was subtle about it, but one by one we started noticing our orders were … odd. We fallen have been growing in numbers pretty quickly ever since."

After I got my fill of dog petting, I straightened up. "Yeah, look. I *need* to make sure Willow's safe. Promise to a late friend, I'm sure you can understand. And this artefact is the only leverage I've got. Nothing personal, but …"

The woman thought for a moment. "Can you give me some sort of guarantee that you'll keep your end of the bargain?"

"Other than acknowledging the fact that backstabbing a pair of fallen angels would probably be a bad idea? Well, I could give you my word as a mage of the Circle. I don't have anything really concrete for you, but I'm a woman of my word."

The angel wrestled with the dilemma for a moment. "Alright. Deal."

I sighed in relief. "Thank you!"

My legs were killing me when I returned to the shelter. Katey was, understandably, deeply worried, but at least the news I could deliver was hopeful. The fallen angels seemed sympathetic to random civilians, so I hoped I could count on them to save Willow. They certainly had the skill. In the meantime, I wrote to Veronica.

Dear Veronica

We were right. I managed to talk to a fallen angel—the same one that saved Ryan a while back—and she confirmed it. Apparently, the Demon Lord managed to take control a bit before the War of Three Truths, and angels have been falling ever since.

Willow's in trouble, but it's a problem I might have already solved. I was looking in that church you shot up for info about fallen angels after I'd heard The One's followers were driven from the city. I think a squad of them came looking for an artefact they'd left in a secret compartment, but I got to it first. I managed to hide from them, but they saw Willow while she was waiting to pick me up in the car. They took her. But a fallen angel came up to me afterwards, and I struck a deal: the artefact in exchange for making sure Willow's safe. A risk, but it seems the fallen angels, these ones at least, are nice enough.

I've been studying the artefact as best I can in my lab. Divine magic isn't my speciality, but I think it's a weapon of some kind, based on conjuration magic. I don't think it's extremely high-yield, so to speak, probably no more than enough to secure a house, if that. I don't have a printer down here, so I can't send you my photos, but I've attached a sketch Katey made; she's remarkably crafty   I miss you, Veronica, and not just because I feel so safe with you around (though you know how much I love watching you kick ass). The feeling of you holding me in your arms gives me indescribable warmth, and I want to feel it again. I dream of a normal life, you and me in comfort. I hope we're able to make a world where that's possible.

Yours,
Sarah

The next day, I headed to the shelter earlier than I normally did, Katey in tow, in the hope that the fallen angels would come through. The artefact was tucked into my bag, and I felt nervous. I doubted anyone was going to try something with a whole crowd around, but I was still carrying something valuable, and visible to those with the eyes to see, and that made me a potential target.

Fortunately, visible anxiety was hardly unusual these days, so no-one looked at me twice. As we waited, we found that something of a board-game club had started up among the survivors. We found something light and easy, just enough to keep our minds occupied. It was surprisingly busy, and the size of the library the group had assembled … I had a feeling it was because no-one was manning the register at the games store. But it was fun.

A few hours passed, and I started to grow bored of the collection. Then, the fallen angel in dog form trotted up to me, tail wagging, getting my attention with a quick *Ruff!*

I allowed a little hope to bloom inside me. "Oh, hey! Any luck with Willow?"

Ruff! The dog barked affirmatively. His tail wagged a little faster and he started to sniff my bag eagerly.

But I wanted to see Willow first. "Where is she?"

The dog moved his paw in the pattern of an 'X'. I blinked, trying to parse what he was trying to tell me. Seeing I didn't understand, the dog looked around before scurrying to a nearby wall. I followed. When I approached, he pawed at a nearby first-aid kit.

"Willow is at …" First-aid course? No, *medical* … "Do you mean the hospital?"

The dog barked excitedly.

That made sense, though it wasn't exactly the best of news. "Alright, guess we're heading to the hospital then… And you really should have sent an angel that can talk to deliver a message." The dog gave a *rrf* that sounded like an agreement.

Katey was looking at me, bemused. "A dog?"

"Oh, yeah, should have mentioned. Angels can choose their forms. This one chose a dog," I said. "Anyway, hospital?"

Upon our arrival, the staff took us to Willow's room. The other fallen was there, leaning on the wall, talking to her. "… lie and say everything's going to be alright. But there's light, here and there. Couple of places where kids are still playing. Look for ____"

Katey immediately ran to her mother, who was lying in bed with a concerning number of casts. Not seriously considering the implications of the casts, Katey ran up to give her mother a hug. "Mum! You're alright!"

Willow grunted. "Ngh … no hugs."

As Katey sheepishly pulled away, the humanoid angel explained, "The Templars 'interrogated' her. Not pretty. But I dispatched them."

Katey enthusiastically shook her hand. "Thank you! Thank you so much!"

The angel grinned. "You're welcome. Speaking of thanks …"

I'd meant what I'd said. I handed the angel the artefact. "As promised."

The angel examined it a moment before stashing it in her trench coat. "Glad for it. Anyway, I have places to be."

The angel stood and turned to leave, pausing a moment while Katey gave the canine angel a number of extremely grateful scratches. As they left, I turned to Willow. "Sorry about, you know …"

Willow seemed to be having trouble speaking. "Not your fault," she murmured eventually.

I wasn't about to let myself off the hook that easy. "I should have done something! Something more than just leave you in the car. I've seen what the Templars are capable of—I should have ——"

Willow interrupted me, shaking her head. "Ten of them, one of you … nothing you could have done."

There was a long pause. "I'm glad you're …" *Alright,* I was about to say. Maybe not. "Safe."

I'd sent Veronica a note straight after we left to let her know that the angels had come through. Her reply came a couple of days later.

Dear Sarah

Glad everything was alright. And Willow's right: it wasn't your fault. All kinds of shit can happen in a warzone. Learning how to adapt to the chaos is one of the biggest lessons you're taught in the army. And there's no way you could have taken on a

At the bottom of the page was a small bloodstain. Not big,
just a drop, but blood nonetheless. And Veronica's handwriting …
in a moment of fear, I took out all of her letters and compared
them in order. And I could see, ever so subtly, Veronica's
handwriting deteriorating.

Veronica was going to burn herself down to nothing.

But this was something I could, just maybe, help with.

*calm, of you and I playing those games we love together, of me
'helping' you work out, of you listening as I drone on about
magic. But if you can find those few days, spend them with me.
    Sarah*

Over time, living in the apocalypse became … normal.
Routine, almost. I managed to get into something of a rhythm in
life. Spending my days creating protective charms for barter and
conjuring food to eat, making regular trips to the shelter to trade
and to catch up with friends, and spending my evenings playing
games with Katey. We visited Willow in the hospital often, and
while her capture by the Templars had scarred her, we gave her
reason to smile.

The barrage of war news started to slow; most factions
had made their opening moves and exhausted large parts of their
forces. It didn't stop, of course. Word came of skirmishes over
vital supplies and the shifting of battle lines. But the chaos was
muted, just a little. With some more stability, a few less-essential
businesses managed to return to the city—bars and hairdressers
and tailors. A brisk trade in salvage cropped up, for both money
and barter.

And Veronica managed to find those few days of leave.

She let me know a week ahead of time, a week I spent
brimming with excitement. We only had a few days, but I made
preparations to ensure we could make the most of the time. With a
bar reopened, I made reservations for a date. I bartered for all
sorts of treats and made sure to catch up on the cleaning. I dug out
my nicer clothes, something I hadn't had occasion to wear for
months.

I was halfway through conjuring some more food when
the bunker's intercom buzzed. I completely forgot about the spell
I was casting, which led to the half-formed mana bursting out in a
gooey explosion all over my lab. I barely noticed in my race to the
bunker door. I repeatedly pressed the *open* button, as if it would
somehow cause the door to open faster.

But, despite what my impatience would say about the
matter, Veronica was before me soon enough. Again, she had
more than a few stitches and bandages scattered across her body,

clearly visible under her plain clothes. But her grin was as casually confident as ever as I squeezed through the half-open bunker door to give her a hug.

Veronica laughed in adoration and surprise at the goo that clung to me. "Uh … puppy?"

I had finally managed to process the half-spell's effects. "Oh. Um, hold on." I pulled away and spent a minute dispelling all the goo that covered me. "Sorry, I was in the middle of making some more food."

After hurriedly cleaning up, I took Veronica into the bedroom. "Alright honey, I know you've been through hell— whether literally or not, I don't know—so I want you to take some time to relax before we have dinner tonight. I've made reservations! But for now, you lie down and relax, and I'll give you another massage."

Veronica chuckled as she lounged on the bed. "Puppy, I came here to spend time with you, not for a resort experience!"

"I'm not sure you can really call one mage improvising during the apocalypse a 'resort', but I'm doing my best."

Apparently, I'd got pretty good at giving massages. Veronica even dozed off after an hour. That caused a pretty difficult dilemma over whether to let her sleep or wake her up in time for our reservation. I reluctantly decided on the latter; she'd have time enough to catch up later.

Veronica didn't have anything fancy to wear, but neither of us minded. As much as Veronica rocked that three-piece suit, she looked just fine in a singlet and cargo pants. It wasn't like formalwear was much of a priority during the apocalypse, anyway. The food was surprisingly good, despite the circumstances (but then, living on conjured food and ration packs probably put a dent in our standards).

We returned to the bunker in high spirits. We broke out my wargaming models, and each of us scored a solid win or two against the other. We played some other board games, inviting Katey to join us. She and Veronica didn't have all that much in common, but we had plenty of fun, the three of us. Then, night fell and the two of us headed to the bedroom. When morning came, neither of us was in a hurry to get up. I only did so because

Veronica was thinking about it, so I hurried to make her breakfast in bed.

For those moments, it was like the apocalypse was far away. Sure, there was a war on. But Veronica had done her part a hundred times over, and humans needed rest. She more than deserved just a day or two to ignore her worries. Perhaps I was contributing to the war for the fate of humanity in my own way: Veronica would fight harder if she was in better condition.

Halfway into Veronica's well-deserved holiday, I called her into my lab. I was a little nervous. "Hey, V … I, uh, was kind of thinking about, you know, what happened, that got you discharged …"

Veronica looked concerned. "I'm not sure how much more I should tell you. Legally, I've already said too much."

"Well, you said all your unit got medals, and I was thinking … well, Katey and I, we …" I retrieved something from a nearby drawer. "We made you this."

It was a homemade medal in a frame with a homemade certificate that read *The GOLDEN HEART is hereby presented to VERONICA WAINWRIGHT for HEROICALLY STANDING UP TO AUTHORITY IN THE FACE OF ATROCITY.*

Veronica's eyes widened as she gingerly took it. "You made this?"

"I mean, Katey did a lot of the work. Scavenged some craft supplies. Managed to find a few ink cartridges for the printer. It's nothing, I just …" I trailed off, not really sure why I had bothered.

When Veronica didn't respond, I looked up at her. She was tearing up. I thought that maybe I had made a mistake, that I might have stirred some memories better forgotten. But then she wrapped me in a tight hug. It took her two or three tries to speak between her sobs. "Thank you, Sarah. Thank you so much."

Chapter Eleven

All too soon, Veronica was called back to her war. I missed her sorely, but at least I wasn't wholly alone; Katey and I kept each other company, Willow was healing over time, and I still had my tabletop roleplaying group, all of whom had grown close in recent months. There was only so much I could do, but I did my best to keep doing my part, if not for the whole war, then for the lives of those surviving it.

One day, on one of my trips to the shelter, the pair of fallen angels approached me again. "Sarah Torren? We need to talk," said the woman.

I slipped my hand into my reagent pouch. "What about?"

Her tone was a touch grim. "It takes a bit of explanation, but look, we're not here to kill you. You have my word on that."

I was very much on guard, but they'd come through for me with Willow, so I trusted them just enough to follow them into a quiet, obscure part of the shelter. The angel explained, "Alright, so word's been starting to spread about what's happened to The One, and after the Thaleites started looking into it, word reached the Arbiter, which is basically in charge of implementing The One's rules. So far, they've been loyalist, but this is a case they're willing to put on trial. If they can be convinced, whole swathes of other loyalists will fall—enough that The One might be vulnerable. And then we can end all this."

"Here comes the 'but'."

"But they're a stickler for the rules and want to confront humanity over starting the apocalypse." The angel folded her arms. "And I understand you had a part in that."

I got defensive. "Okay, first of all, no-one *told me* that killing an angel in heaven would trigger the apocalypse. Second of all, the angel was shooting at us *from heaven*, so even an angel should have expected us to shoot back."

The fallen sighed. "Look, I'm not here to blame you. But the Arbiter wants to put humanity on trial, along with you, for your part in starting the apocalypse."

This didn't sound good. "What does this … 'trial' involve?"

"We'll take you to the Court of Souls, on the edge of the celestial realm. Your … accomplice will be there, and the Thaleites have some old deals in place meaning they can send a representative. Then we talk to the Arbiter. If we're lucky, we'll convince them that humanity is doing its best, that your actions were justified. And deal with their judgement."

"If we're not lucky?"

The angel didn't sugarcoat it. "Then you'll be cast down to hell. I can't force you to show up. But it's still our best chance at ending all this."

I knew what I had to do. Committing to that decision, however, took strength I didn't have in me, not in that moment. "I … need to think about it."

The angel frowned but nodded. "Alright. I'll be around."

I ruminated about the trial for a long time. The concept terrified me. The chance of not just death but being cast down to hell, the domain of demons, where souls were considered merely a resource … but risking my life and soul could save billions of lives. *Billions*. I could save humanity itself. I knew, objectively, that I had to put my soul on the line. I spent the next night mustering the courage.

I was tense as a bowstring the whole of the next morning. As soon as I was ready, I hurried to the shelter as best I could with the weight of my decision weighing down my every step. When I arrived, there was no sign of the fallen angels. I paced around the shelter anxiously, even as my mind groped for a justification to back down.

After a long, torturous hour, the angels approached. "You wanted to see us?"

I mustered my strength and forced the words out of my throat. "I'll do it."

The angel smiled, though it was tempered with the gravity of the situation. "Good. I'll make the arrangements. I've got a portal to the place picked out and secured; just need to co-ordinate with the Arbiter and the Thaleites. Everything should be ready to go in a few days. I'll keep you in the loop."

I nodded, the tension shifting from something immediate to something more distant, but far greater.

I spent the next few days trying to not think about the trial and, for the most part, failing. Even as my mind groped for other subjects to ponder, my train of thought kept returning to the trial. There was so much uncertainty, so many possible scenarios, so many possible outcomes. Some would save humanity. Others meant unimaginable agony (which my mind still speculated about, despite my best efforts to stop it). The matter was only worsened by the circumstances demanding I take some time to get my affairs in order, in case of the worst. At least that only meant deciding who'd get my belongings should the worst come to pass, as well as writing a few letters I hoped wouldn't be sent. Time lost all meaning as one moment of fear led into the next.

Finally, the day came. I was almost relieved. We'd arranged for Veronica and the Thaleites to pick me up directly from the bunker. I was prepared when the intercom buzzed, and I opened the door with a trembling hand. At least it was Veronica on the other side, wearing her power armour, helmet by her side. She seemed just as worried as I, but she forced her expression into a smile. "Hey," she said quietly.

"Hey."

We couldn't find anything more to say. So, we turned, left the bunker and climbed into a waiting transport. A couple of other power-armoured Thaleites were inside, along with an older man with grey-blue eyes in an immaculate suit. The man raised an eyebrow as I took a seat. He spoke with a thick German accent, "You're the one that helped Veronica fire a grenade launcher into heaven?"

As I nodded awkwardly, Veronica introduced us. "Sir, this is Veronica, research mage of the Circle of Magi. Sarah, this is Eckehard Vogel, chairman of the Thaleite Council."

I felt like Frodo sitting at the table with Gandalf and Elrond: far too small to be with people so important. "Um, hi."

As the transport drove off, I rose from my seat and sat on Veronica's heavily armoured lap. Honestly, it wasn't all that comfortable, but that was nothing compared to the raging turmoil in my heart. And it kept me as close as possible to Veronica, giving me that small fragment of warmth I so direly needed. Veronica held me gently, careful not to crush me with the armour's bulk but desiring the closeness as much as I did.

I felt nauseous as the transport rolled along. I wasn't sure how much time it took, only that it was far too long. But the transport finally rolled to a stop, and we exited. We found ourselves in front of a ruined church in the suburbs. The fallen angels, with a couple of companions also in human form, were waiting for us. The woman in the trench coat seemed to be the de facto leader. "Afternoon," she greeted us. "As much as I'd like to make introductions, I think we'd all prefer to get this over and done with."

The nerves alone had left me out of breath. "Yes, yes, please."

The angels nodded and beckoned us into the ruins of the church. Where the back rooms used to be, there was a large gold arch, big enough for a set of double doors. The angel spoke an incantation and a portal appeared, leading into a starry expanse. The angel took a deep breath then walked inside, followed by her companions. I walked up to the threshold of the portal. I hesitated. I looked up at Veronica. She gave me a nod, her expression set in resolve. I entered.

The celestial realm was vast. Paths were woven from aurora, arcing in an architectural symphony between ivory platforms suspended in a stellar expanse. Angels, forged from gold and gems, flew in patterns, cogs in a divine machine. A pair of sentries guarded the portal, resplendent pillars with eyes tracking our every move. The fallen angel acknowledged them with a nod, addressing one. "Kezriel. Been a while."

A band of angels approached, led by one in human form wearing a plain robe. "You are here for your trial. Follow." With no further word, the angels turned and started leading us down the path. Eyes, countless eyes, were on us every step of the way.

Veronica paused just for a moment, donning her helmet before marching on with us.

At least our destination wasn't far. We were in a large amphitheatre, which my mind unhelpfully compared to a coliseum. There was a podium just off-centre, at which another angel floated, two massive eyes held on scales, gavels floating around them. The humans and fallen stood in front of it as angelic sentries hovered around us.

The judge spoke with calm gravity. "Let all know this: my gaze pierces all lies and illusions. Let none be spoken, lest the lying tongue be cast out. Let the trial commence. Sinner, you who are christened Veronica Wainwright, you bear the weight of the defilement of heaven on your soul. How do you stand against these charges?"

Veronica stood firm. "It was self-defence, and ignorance. An angel was firing at me from the portal. I didn't know about the rules of the apocalypse, so as far as I was concerned, I had every right to return fire."

The judge betrayed little emotion, save perhaps a shred of contempt for Veronica's actions. "Do you repent for your sins?"

Veronica considered her answer carefully. "If I'd known that killing the angel in heaven would have caused the apocalypse, I wouldn't have done it. As I said, ignorance. But I didn't know that. So, I place the responsibility on all who failed to tell me."

"You do not recognise the sanctity of heaven?" the judge asked, and it felt accusatory.

The fallen angel leader, still in human form, interrupted. "Amrikeal—judge—I have some relevant evidence."

"Speak."

"As you know, ever since the 7th Arbitration—and the conflict that resulted, which the humans call the War of Three Truths—human–angel conflicts have been steadily rising. Thaleite records indicate that human casualties, including non-combatants and those ignorant of the supernatural, have become almost commonplace. They consistently match, or are at least very close to, what records I've found in the lands of the dead. I posit that this would obviously cause humans to lose their faith in heaven."

The judge said, "I reject your statement, Semriel. Those deaths were for the greater good."

The fallen, presumably Semriel, countered, "But if The One has been ——"

"Silence." The judge returned their attention to Veronica. "Answer, Veronica: Do you recognise the sanctity of heaven?"

"I've never been deployed there, for obvious reasons," Veronica explained. "I've never given the matter much thought."

Chairman Vogel raised his hand. "May I make a suggestion?"

Only the judge's eyes moved, locking on to the Chairman. "You are not on the record."

"Chairman Vogel, leader of the Thaleites. You'll find I have maximum-level diplomatic authority, per the Treaty of Rome, section 4c." The chairman showed the judge a tattoo on his wrist, a complex rune I didn't recognise.

A small cherub in the form of a fish briefly examined the rune before whispering to the judge. The judge then said, "You authority is recognised, Chairman Vogel. You may speak."

"The Thaleites would be willing to officially recognise the sanctity of heaven, and all rules of engagement regarding angels and their supporters are open to negotiation. However, that would, at a minimum, require your co-operation regarding ending the apocalypse." Chairman Vogel spoke with impressive calm, circumstances being what they were.

The judge considered this for I couldn't tell how long. Tense as I was, it could have been a second or an hour. "For this, I must know you are pure."

Semriel snapped, "Can't you see!? Are you so blinded by procedure ——"

"Silence, or be held in contempt, and condemned," the judge intoned. It then glowed, and the shape of a massive broadsword glowed in the air, solidifying in front of Veronica. "There is one way to show your purity. Kill your accomplice."

I froze. My heart plummeted into the depths. Slowly, all eyes turned to me. For the first time since I had met her, Veronica sounded scared. "I … please, there *has* to be another way."

Chairman Vogel stepped forward. "If I may, judge, I know that you accept the transfer of sin. I would be willing to serve as a scapegoat for both of these women and take punishment in their stead."

The judge's voice turned a touch quizzical. "Why?"

Vogel took a deep breath. "Because I've seen too many innocent people die already. I admit, in command, I've done some things I'm not proud of. When I became a Thaleite, I took an oath to defend human lives. If the cost of saving humanity must be a life … I've sacrificed enough of other people's lives. It's time I sacrifice my own."

"That would have no purpose. The purpose is to show humanity may yet achieve the standards set for it, as it has failed to so far. The mortal must ascend past lust and do their duty to all." The judge's voice was utterly matter-of-fact.

I knew exactly what the right thing to do was. My life, for humanity? The choice was blatantly obvious. Hell, I'd seen this in all sorts of media countless times before: the hero sacrificing themselves for the greater good. Applauded it, even fantasised about it once or twice. And it wasn't like it would be hard. All I had to do was give Veronica a nod. Tell her it was okay. Tell her it was the right thing to do, that I was willing to give my life for humanity.

I couldn't move. Couldn't speak, couldn't nod. I just froze. I tried to shape the words in my mouth, just a simple *go ahead*, but my throat wouldn't give them form. A deep, animal drive to survive took over, and I didn't have the strength to override it. Did my cowardice really outweigh my compassion?

Veronica stared at me for a long while as I trembled. I couldn't see her expression through her visor. She glanced at the chairman. "Orders, sir?" *Take this decision from me.*

"At your discretion, commander." *I don't want it either.*

She took the sword in one hand, her gaze running up and down the blade. She slowly removed her helmet. She was crying. She walked up to me. Held the blade against my throat.

The thoughts echoed in my mind. *Tell her it's okay! Tell her you're willing! Tell her …* But I was scared. So scared.

Veronica looked me in the eye. I saw a deep love there. I realised, there and then, I meant *so much* to her. I made her happy.

Her expression shifted, brow furrowing in resolve.

She raised the sword to swing.

And drove it into the judge.

The judge screamed, cracked and fractured as the blade turned black. As the angels screamed in protest, Veronica pulled a machine gun from her back and opened fire, gunning down three before they had any time to react. As more swooped down, she stood between me and them, unleashing ballistic wrath.

The fallen angels and Thaleites realised the fight had started and the actions could be debated later. All drew weapons and fired on the oncoming horde (save the canine-form angel, who simply eviscerated one of the ones that got close). Even Vogel joined in the fight with a pistol, though he quickly ducked behind his power-armoured guards.

After the first wave was dispatched, Veronica donned her helmet again. She turned to the others. "We're getting out of here. Kill any of the feathered bastards that get in our way."

Vogel was composed enough that I suspected that this wasn't the first time one of his meetings had suddenly ended with gunfire. "I can agree with the first part. Let's get going."

A series of massive pillars materialised around the court, and barriers of golden light formed between them. More angels started gathering beyond them. Veronica punched the barriers; they flickered briefly but held. Semriel raced to the base of one of the pillars. "Wouldn't have mentioned this system if … look, mage, come here. We can bypass it. Everyone else, keep the others occupied."

No-one else had a better plan, so I hurried to Semriel's side. With a strike, she revealed some golden patterns beneath the pillars. "Alright, if you can shift mana, there's an exploit …" She quickly explained the basic structure of the spell, and how it could be sabotaged by a mage in the right place in the right time. Meanwhile, the second wave of angels attacked. Veronica seemed almost happy about this, her rage driving kill after kill. Only a couple even got close, and they didn't last long against the lighter-armed of those assembled.

The magical hacking took a minute, and a lot of effort, but we managed it. One of the barriers flickered and died. Semriel called, "Alright, time to ——"

She had to stop talking because she was too busy rolling out of the way of a massive blast of holy fire. A titanic angel descended from on high, a glowing orb of fire whose rings were wreathed in lightning. Veronica didn't hesitate. She brandished the sword, now blackened by the sin it was being used for, and charged. The new angel fired a torrent of lightning and fire at Veronica. With inhuman speed, she dodged into cover behind the pillars before leaping back out. She leapt on to another angel as it swooped to attack, driving her sword into its core before propelling herself off its corpse towards its larger comrade. Her first strike took a chunk out of one of its rings as it screamed in protest. The angel fired back. Veronica shifted into a defensive position but still took a hit.

It looked serious, but Veronica barely seemed to notice. With mythic athletics, she bounded between the platforms, bridges and her target. She evaded its barrage of attacks, diving in to slash at it whenever it showed an opening before ducking back, taking the chance to take out a few of the angels trying to enter the fight.

Meanwhile, I was hiding behind one of the intact barriers. Panic had driven me to cover, and the more rational parts of my mind helpfully offered that in a fight involving fallen angels and power-armoured super-soldiers, I would probably only get in the way anyway. A few of the angels took shots at me, but my danger-sensing ring and magical wards held just enough for me to only take a few winding hits. One of the perks of not being much of a threat.

Veronica obviously didn't need my help. She shattered the titanic angel's rings, one by one. Finally, she leapt into the air and drove the sword straight into its core. The angel screamed, shattering. The other angels only seemed further enraged. Veronica only saw a target-rich environment. She cut a swathe through the celestial legions. Countless angels fired on her, but only a handful landed hits, and only a couple of those seemed to cause damage. Damage that would have killed most people, but Veronica had left 'most people' far behind.

The rest of us realised that Veronica had given us an opening, so we took it. The other Thaleite soldiers had arranged themselves around the chairman (he'd taken a hit, but the severity of the wound compared to the creatures firing at him made me suspect his suit wasn't ordinary cloth), and I decided that that was probably the safest place. With some more mobile cover, I even managed to help, just a little, conjuring the occasional barrier to deflect the odd blast that came our way. We kept moving, making our way to the walkways, creeping in Veronica's wake. Countless fragments of soulstuff rained from the sky as angel after angel fell.

Hearts racing, we managed to make our way to the portal back home (despite me nearly tripping on all the spent bullet casings more than once). Sentries formed around it, but Veronica obliterated them with a barrage of grenades. Veronica stood nearby, holding them off as we rushed through.

On the other side, one of the Thaleite soldiers asked the chairman, "Destroy the portal, sir?" When the chairman nodded, he pulled out some explosives. As he set them up, he called through the portal, "Wainwright! We're through, get back here!"

There was a pause. Then, Veronica emerged from the portal. Her helmet had been blown off, revealing her blood-streaked face. My mind was a battleground of my own emotions, including various degrees of fear, guilt and concern. Despite her obviously grave wounds, Veronica spun around, hefting her machine gun and firing a few bursts through the portal. Her comrade finished setting the explosives, shouting, "Alright, let's clear out!"

I needed no further incentive to hurry back into the transport, where I was soon joined by the others. Vogel called to the driver, "Hospital, double-time!" The transported roared off to the sound of explosives detonating behind us.

Then, the world was noisy, in a silent way. The ringing in my ears. The pounding of my heart. The roar of the engine. The pants of exhaustion. No-one said anything. We were all trying to figure out what to say.

Vogel managed to find something, after a while. "Wainwright, get your armour off so you don't have to in the middle of the hospital."

"I'm fine, sir," she said, and if I'd only had her tone to go by, I would've believed it.

Vogel wasn't in the mood to argue. "Commander, you're getting medical attention at the hospital. That's an order."

When we arrived, Veronica's wounds were obviously severe enough to see her admitted swiftly. But a squad of power-armoured soldiers in an armoured vehicle quickly drew hospital management down, and they briefly argued with Vogel. He said that while he'd be keeping all the Thaleite's wargear and wouldn't allow anyone to be surrendered to the authorities, he'd compensate the hospital for the use of medical supplies and time. Vogel was a charismatic man, and the hospital manager decided she was not willing to argue with someone with power-armoured bodyguards.

I sat down on a chair in the waiting room, trying to process the events of the last hour, with little success. After Vogel finished negotiating with management, one of his guards turned to him. "A question, sir?"

"Yes?"

"Why didn't you order the commander to kill the mage?" he asked. I felt like I was going to be sick.

Vogel frowned at his soldier. "We can discuss that in full when we're not in public … but do you really expect me to order one of my soldiers to kill the woman she loves?"

The soldier didn't seem satisfied. "We took an oath ——"

Vogel said forcefully *"Later*, soldier. Later."

As the Thaleites (sans Veronica) left, Semriel sat down beside me. "Well … that didn't go to plan."

My voice trembled. "What happens now?"

She sighed. "Things get ugly, that's what. Maybe not straight away—your girlfriend took out some serious names back there. But the angels won't let this go unanswered."

I was blinking back tears. "She should have killed me."

Semriel didn't say anything.

Chapter Twelve

Time had lost all meaning that day. I simply waited tearfully until I could see Veronica. I could take some small comfort in the fact that seeing someone weeping in a hospital was hardly noteworthy. I felt like my guilt had opened a yawning void in my heart that I could just collapse into.

Finally, a nurse said I could see Veronica. I followed her to a room where Veronica was sitting in a bed. Despite the sheer number of bandages covering her (which had become terrifyingly normal for her), I could see anger in her eyes, a plan to visit a bloody vengeance on her enemies. I leapt at her, wrapping my arms around her and crying. She immediately relaxed. "Hey, hey. I'm here. I'm alright."

I had a lot to say, and this time the only obstacle was shaping my words around my sobs. "I- I'm so sorry."

Veronica seemed baffled. "What for?"

"I-I should have let you … I should have told you it was okay, let you kill me."

Veronica whispered, "What?"

I wailed, "People are going to die! Because of me!"

Veronica took my head in her hands, pulling my gaze towards her. "Look at me, puppy. I'm the one who made that decision. Not you."

"I knew what you had to do, what was right, but I was scared." I couldn't see her face through my tears.

"It wouldn't have changed anything, Sarah."

When I looked at her, confused, she explained, "I've seen more than my fair share of corpses in my time. Made too damn many. I can't see yours. I won't."

We held each other for a long time.

News from the outside world picked up in intensity again. It only took a couple of days for the angels to muster a massive and brutal counterattack aimed at humanity, and the other factions vying for Earth were all too happy to take advantage of our weakness. In the meantime, I visited Veronica every day. The hospital didn't have the resources for luxuries, so I brought some every day (and a few for Willow).

After a couple of days, I entered Veronica's room to find her sitting on her bed, scowling. She brightened when she saw me, but only a little. "Hey, puppy."

"What's up?" I asked, as if the apocalypse hadn't brought everyone reason aplenty to be in a bad mood.

She grumbled, "My people are fighting over what I did. Half of them want me dismissed …" As she trailed off, my heart sunk. Then, Veronica looked straight at me. "Don't blame yourself. You're not *allowed* to blame yourself." She resumed, "Anyway, I'm not getting any new deployments until enough people finally agree." She shook her head. "Doesn't help that the chairman's getting a lot of flak, too. They say he should have ordered me."

I wondered if, had he given the order, she would have carried it out. I decided neither of us wanted the answer to that question.

The next day, I managed to bring a handful of our wargaming models and conjured a table for a small skirmish game. The magic was tricky, but the delighted look on Veronica's face when I pulled it off was more than worth it. I ended up beating her pretty soundly, but she didn't mind.

As I packed up, she leaned close. "Sarah … can you conjure me weapons and armour?"

I hesitated. "Not the kind of wargear you're used to, and it won't last for extended periods. But give me a day or two, I could make you a knife and a few protective charms," I explained. "Are you going to …?"

I saw a fire in Veronica's eyes. "I'm not going to just sit here while people argue over whether I should have murdered the woman I love. Demons and angels are trying to burn the Earth. I need to stop them."

I was deeply worried about her, but she had a point: the battle for the fate of the planet had taken a turn for the worse, and a super-soldier like her could be decisive. So, I got to work. I took my time. When I mentioned to my friends that Veronica was going back into the field on her own, Ryan revealed something surprising: during his time as a vampire's thrall, he'd met some contacts for the black market. With all the fighting, there were more than a few weapons being lost on battlefields, which fell into the hands of canny scavengers. Ryan passed this on to Veronica, who was happy to pay the hefty price for some under-the-table hardware. Prices were made more manageable by my protective charms, as they were of particular value to the kinds of people that operated on the black market.

So, one day, Veronica met me in the bunker to equip herself. It was nothing compared to what she would have been issued by the Thaleites, but I'd seen what she could do with a single pistol. With a gun, some charms and a nice big knife, she could cause no small amount of carnage. She had also kept the executioner's blade from the trial; her using it on the judge had somehow warped it, severing it from The One's will, but like a fallen angel, it had kept its terrible power. She named it Wrath.

Her departure was delayed, of course, by the two of us taking a long moment to hold each other close. I slowly and softly ran my arms across her, feeling her warmth, the curve of her muscles, the texture of her scars, committing all of her to memory.

I whispered, "Kick their asses, honey."

It wasn't long before word spread of a one-woman crusade against the forces of heaven and hell. Without the Thaleites' direction, Veronica simply headed to the nearest concentration of The One's followers, and she killed. People started referring to her as the Reaper. I kept my ears open for any rumours and found many. Some of them strange, some of them impressive, and some of them contradicting other rumours. With Veronica's legendary prowess, it was difficult to sift the truth from the fiction.

Dark questions drifted in and out of my mind, only mitigated by my efforts to survive. The trial was the subject of many, though not all. Was it moral to let a war keep going to spare a single life? How much blood was on my hands because of my cowardice? Did that make me a killer? Did I deserve to be safely ensconced in a bunker while people died? Should I be doing more? What more *could* I do?

In the meantime, I did my best to keep living. It was hard, from time to time, the angels' counterattack having dampened much of the new hope among the survivors. I was also still wrestling with the question of what I should have done at the trial. But I still managed to live, for Veronica's sake if nothing else.

I was much more motivated when I found another letter from Veronica.

Dear Sarah

I'm making them pay. Took out a camp of evangelicals yesterday and restocked on their munitions. Managed to take out a few angels while I was at it. I won't stop until humanity is saved, even if I'm the only one fighting.

No idea what's going to be left when the dust finally settles, but more than anything, I want something to be left for you. On day, I want you to look up and see the sky is blue again. I want you to enjoy yourself, have one of those ice creams you like so much, not a care in the world. I'll keep fighting until that's your future. Even if I never see it.

I love you.

Veronica Wainwright

The painful part was I couldn't reply. I'd skipped over learning how to summon messenger pigeons (I'd thought that, with the internet, it'd be redundant—a pre-apocalypse way of thinking), and even if I could work out that spell, a pigeon arriving at the wrong moment would risk exposing Veronica's position. I would have sent a message through the Thaleites, but she wasn't working with them, so they probably had little idea of where she was. So, I couldn't let her know I was alright. Couldn't let her know how much I missed her. Couldn't let her know that all I wanted in my future was her.

It wasn't the last letter, but they grew less frequent, shorter, and steadily coated in more of her blood. Then, after a few weeks, the letters stopped. There were many reasons it could have happened. None of them good. Was Veronica still even alive? Reports of the Reaper were increasingly sparse. I lay awake at night, wondering what Veronica was doing. Agonising over the possibilities.

After nearly two weeks of no word, the bunker's intercom buzzed. Holding tight to the thin strand of hope that remained, I rushed to the door. I stopped myself from opening it straight away, instead opening a connection to the other side. "Hello?"

The voice was unfamiliar. "Excuse me, I'm looking for Sarah Torren."

"Who is it?"

"Jonah Warrington, Thaleite Intelligence. I'd like a word with you regarding Veronica Wainwright," she said. My heart raced, suspended between hope and despair. I opened the door.

Jonah was revealed to be a stocky woman in a plain suit. "Miss Torren, you're Commander Wainwright's partner, aren't you?"

My voice was wavering. "Um, yeah. Is something …?"

"She's not KIA, if that's what you're wondering." I sighed in relief as she continued, "But the situation is … complicated." She relaxed slightly. "About a month ago, she grew impatient with command and left to engage on her own campaign, hunting angels. Thaleite command has started giving her deployments, all of which she's accepted, but she remains unsatisfied. When not on a mission, she fights angels of her own accord, and command hasn't been able to stop her."

I fidgeted awkwardly. "I think she was pretty unhappy after the trial, with … everything."

Jonah's voice remained level. "Yes, I … my thoughts on the matter aren't relevant. What's important is that the commander's condition is deteriorating steadily. Her combat performance is dropping, and she's been taking injuries that she's refused to have treated. This is where you come in. The Thaleites have never shied away from unconventional solutions to problems, and her squadmates report that you have some influence on her."

I put two and two together. "You want me to tell her to take a break?"

"That's the short version. The logistics of that will prove more difficult; we believe her radio was damaged in a recent engagement, so we're doing something more creative. We have reason to believe that the angels are staging a massive attack on the city. Veronica is close enough to intervene, so we're sending her as much information on the attack as we can, though we're not sure how much she's receiving. Given her current anger at the angels, if she gets enough information, her presence will be almost guaranteed."

"So I show up to the fight and talk her into getting some rest?"

Jonah nodded. "Exactly. I can't tell you everything, but command believes there'll be a large escalation soon, and when that happens, they want Veronica in top condition."

I thought about the logistics of the problem. "Alright, I'm going to need somewhere more-or-less safe that's close enough to where she'll be, so I can duck down there while the fight's going on. I might also need to have a doctor willing to come down to the bunker when I call."

The agent nodded. "Sounds reasonable. I'll pass that up the chain. Here." She handed me a radio. "The broadcast is encrypted using Thaleite diplomatic channels; it'll let you talk to our staff."

I took the radio. "Sure."

Jonah stood a bit straighter. "Excellent. We'll make the preparations and be in touch. Good luck, Miss Torren."

I'd heard enough gunshots for a hundred lifetimes, but I could handle a few more if it was for Veronica. I daubed every defensive rune I knew on my clothes, and one or two directly on my skin. I prepared a number of spells, some to help me take care of Veronica, others to help keep me safe.

I arrived at the shelter to see the hurried readying of fortifications and dozens of Thaleite soldiers standing alongside the authorities. I'd gathered that there was some tension between the Thaleites and the authorities, but fortunately they'd set aside whatever differences they had in the face of a greater threat. As I approached, I was quickly accosted by some policemen, who started herding me into the more heavily fortified basements of the shelter where the rest of the civilians were cowering. After some awkwardly navigated conversations, I was spotted by Jonah, who informed the police that I was with them. They looked at the Thaleite suspiciously but let her guide me away and into a waiting armoured vehicle, this one with a flak cannon mounted on top of it. "Stay inside, drop a few spells if you can, but most importantly, *stay alive*," she said. "It's preferable that we know where you are."

"I promise, staying alive was already pretty high on the list of priorities."

Jonah snorted. "Glad to hear it. Good luck. We're counting on you."

As she walked off, I decided to make myself useful by painting a few protective runes onto the hull of the vehicle, with the driver's approval. I stuck to basic ones, hoping that every little bit might help. It gave me something productive to do, at any rate. As I worked, something occurred to me: I was very important to the fate of the world, to the point that I was a central part of a plan concocted by an international organisation of monster hunters. And I'd found myself in that position because humanity's greatest warrior had a thing for tiny dorks who infodumped. I … had absolutely no idea what to make of all that.

Only a few minutes later, I saw all the soldiers scramble for their fortifications. One of the vehicle's crew called to me, "Here they come!" It was all I needed to hear to dive for the relative safety of an armoured and warded hull. A second later, the battlefield echoed with the thunder of guns. I was getting used to it over time, but it was never comfortable. After a moment, though, I started to resent my own uselessness, and so I peered out of a nearby hatch to examine the fight. From the defensive position, it was hard to see much over the huge raining comets of heavenly fire interspersed with black clouds of flak. So, I did what little I could, summoning barriers to weaken the raining holy fire.

There was a blast, and the vehicle fell on its side. I was flung from where I was crouched and fell painfully on my side. My protective wards were enough to prevent my dislocating or breaking anything, but it was hardly a comfortable landing. Then, I could smell smoke. I was scrambling to my feet and rushing out of the transport even before I felt my danger ring thrum. As the vehicle erupted into flames behind me, a surge of adrenaline propelled me towards the first building I saw.

My ring thrummed again, and I filled my wards with power. A blast of holy fire impacted just beside me, shattering my wards and flinging me to the side. Without my wards to cushion my fall, I hit concrete hard. I cried out, my head throbbing in pain and my side burning with a graze. Too disorientated to stand, I started to crawl. Then an angel landed in front of me. I froze.

I heard Veronica roar in rage, tackling it as she drove her defiled sword through its core. It hadn't even started to dissipate as she rolled off it, raising a machine gun to the sky. Her armour was pitted with burns, and she was without her helmet, showing a face streaked with blood and soot and set in an angry snarl. Her eyes blazed with rage as she sent her ballistic wrath back up into the sky. When some angels landed around her, she effortlessly shifted back to melee, somersaulting around the angel's strikes before cutting them to pieces.

When that wave of angels was dispatched, she turned to me. As I tried to stand, she rushed to me, scooping me up before sprinting with inhuman speed to a nearby building and setting me down before I could really process was happening. Then, she immediately turned back towards the fight. As I caught my breath, I peered outside, watching her fight. She proved herself more than worthy of the title of Reaper. The heavenly fire raining from the sky was joined by dying angels.

Finally, The One's forces got the message. Those few remaining fled. I saw Veronica check the ammunition she carried on her belt before striding after them. I called after her, "Veronica!"

She stopped. I could see her weighing up her lust for battle with her care for me. To my relief, care won. She turned again and walked back up to me. "Puppy … are you alright?"

I winced. "Sore, very sore … but not as bad as you look."

Veronica scoffed. "Scrapes. I'm fine."

I internally estimated the kind of impact that would be needed to make a dent in power armour. I didn't have to know much about armour to know Veronica had to have taken some serious hits. "Honey, why don't we let the medics take a look? At the both of us? I don't want them wasting anything on me that you might need."

"I don't need ——"

"Please?" I whimpered.

Veronica sighed. "Fine."

The two of us staggered over to a nearby truck emblazoned with the red cross. A handful of medics were dealing with much more than a handful of wounded, but Veronica was thrust to the front of the line. She was about to object, but I shut it down with a stern look. As the medic examined her wounds, he swore. "How the *fuck* are you still alive? The only people I've seen covered in this much of their own blood have been dead."

Veronica shrugged. "Grit."

One of the other medics raised an eyebrow. "You can't 'grit' your way out of blood loss."

The other added, "There's only so much I can do. You need to get to hospital as soon as we're done here."

Veronica leaned back. "Too busy for that, I'm afraid. Angels need killing."

The medic exclaimed, "Too busy!? Any of these hits should have killed you!"

"But they didn't." Veronica smirked. "I'll be fine."

I half-whispered, "Veronica? I worry about you."

"Sarah, as I said, I'm fine." She sounded frustrated.

"Look, I hope you're fine. But when you're not around, I keep wondering how you're doing, and seeing you like this—I don't want this to be the last I see of you." I couldn't help but feel a bit manipulative, but then again, everything I was saying was the truth. When Veronica fell silent, I continued, "If you really don't want to go to hospital or something, maybe you could take a day or two? Stay with me? You can rest, and make sure I don't have a concussion or something from that fall?"

Veronica drummed a finger on her armoured thigh, struggling with the decision. "There are more angels out there."

To my surprise, a half-giggle slipped out. "Not that many more, thanks to you. And you're not the only one fighting. Just a few days. I need some rest too. And it'd be easier with you."

One of the medics seemed to be thinking along the same lines. "And if she does have a concussion, which is likely, she could use someone else with her."

Veronica's shoulders slumped. "Fine."

I smiled widely. "Thank you!"

After the medics made sure Veronica's innards weren't about to fall out, she returned her wargear to the Thaleites for repairs—much needed—and then we headed back to the bunker. Off the battlefield, Veronica's strain was starting to show, though I suspected it was just because she was now allowing herself to show it. Regardless, I didn't want to count on her opting for sleep of her own accord. "I'm really tired … and sore. Maybe we could lie down for a while?"

It worked. "Yeah, sure." Veronica plopped herself down on my bed, and I gently rested myself down on top of her. I certainly wasn't complaining about the chance to just lie down, to say nothing of the chance to cuddle Veronica, but I kept myself alert. I had a plan, and a crucial part of it centred around being awake while Veronica slept.

For a while, I wondered if I'd made a tactical mistake. It was proving difficult to keep myself alert while cuddling Veronica, and she took longer than I expected to doze off. I supposed I should have accounted for the fact that it was still morning. But it finally happened. Veronica's breathing slowed and deepened, and she started to snore. I moved to the next phase of the plan: making it as hard as possible for her to get out from under me without waking me. I really wasn't sure how to do that, but I kept my stance wide and tucked the duvet tight underneath us to minimise her manoeuvrability.

The plan worked. I wasn't sure if I dozed off, spaced out or just lost track of time, but I was jolted back into alertness by Veronica attempting to slide herself out from under me. As she did so, I shifted more of my weight onto her torso. She paused, taking a moment to stroke my hair. For a second, I hoped that I didn't need to do any more, but then Veronica whispered, "Puppy, I need to get back into the field."

I looked up and gave her a sad, pleading look. "Veronica, you need to rest."

Veronica sighed in frustration. "I keep telling everyone, I'm fine!"

"And medical experts keep telling you you're not!" I slowly sat up. "Veronica, please …"

Veronica gritted her teeth. "The demons aren't resting, nor are the angels. I can't afford to sit on my ass all day."

"You can't afford to go back!" My voice raised a half-octave in pitch. "Veronica, look at yourself—your guts are being held in with string!"

"It'll hold," Veronica said dismissively.

"What if it doesn't? Veronica, I—" I blinked back tears, "—do you have any idea how terrifying it was to see a drop of your blood on a letter!? If you go back out there like this, I …" My voice dropped to a whisper, "I won't see you again."

Veronica's tone turned angry. "Do you have that little faith in me?"

Tears started to slide down my cheeks. "I have faith in the medics, and the Thaleites. They told me to make sure you got your rest!"

Veronica did at least pause. But then, she lifted me off her. "Dammit, these things need to die!"

I grabbed her arm. "It'll wait! Veronica, please, I can't lose you. Just stay here. A week or two. Let yourself heal. For me?" Veronica stood, but then she hesitated. I whispered, "*Please. I could make you breakfast, or every meal of the day. Get you anything you want. Veronica, you're my hero. You've saved my life, more than once. Saved gods know how many. Please, can you save yourself?"*

Veronica clenched her teeth again. "I can't stay forever."

"As soon as the doctors give you the okay, go ahead. I'll be happy then. You know how much I like seeing you kick ass. But if you die …"

Veronica looked at me for a long while. I would say I tried to look scared for her, but I already was. I needed only make sure the emotion was expressed. After a long pause, Veronica slowly returned to bed. I nearly laughed with relief. "Thank you."

Veronica returned to a casual tone. "I want something to eat, though."

I leapt to my feet. "Anything at all!"

"Even a cake?"

Katey called from up the hall, "There's a bakery in the suburbs that's reopened. I could run there and grab something."

I called back, "Go ahead!" After hearing the bunker door open and close, I turned back to Veronica. "Anything else?"

"You."

I was happy to oblige.

The next morning, I again woke up before Veronica. Once again, I lay there for a long while, feeling Veronica's chest gently rise and fall with her breath. I wondered how long it had been since she had slept. I wondered how long it had been since she'd allowed herself any rest at all.

Eventually, she awoke, smiling as she saw me. "Morning." She started to gently stroke my hair.

As much as I wanted to simply lie down and indulge in her touch, I had work to do. "Alright, V, you just lie down here. I'll get you breakfast."

Veronica started to sit up. "What is it, Valentine's Day?"

I quickly got out of bed, firmly placing my hand on her shoulder. "It's you've-been-getting-blasted-by-angels-for-weeks-straight day. Now, you lie down and relax while I get you breakfast."

Unfortunately, the bunker's meagre supplies meant I couldn't prepare anything all that interesting, but Veronica appreciated the gesture at any rate. I took care of the clean-up before returning to bed to cuddle Veronica. That made her much more inclined to stay in bed.

I was very busy over the next few days. It took a lot of food to keep a super-soldier's frame up, so it took more than a few runs out of the bunker to satisfy her appetite. One of the Thaleites' doctors arrived, and I managed to convince Veronica to let herself be examined through careful alternation between a stern voice and puppy-dog eyes. The doctor, like most medical professionals, was surprised Veronica was even *alive*, and gave Veronica strict instructions to stay in bed as much as possible over the next few days. Or rather, she gave me strict instructions to give Veronica strict instructions to stay in bed.

That part actually proved to be much easier than I initially feared it would be. Now she'd come to terms with not being in the field, Veronica wasn't so fussed with exactly what she was doing in the meantime, and it only took a few cute looks and careful choice of pyjamas to give her what incentive she needed to stay in bed. We happily worked through our collection of movies, and when that started to run dry, Katey was happy to dig up some more. More than that, now she wasn't running on adrenaline and rage, I think she started to realise she was in pain. While I didn't *like* seeing her shoulders sagged and body exhausted, I took it as a hopeful sign that she was finally allowing herself to rest.

And the worst of it faded over time. As days turned into weeks, I saw her smile come more naturally to her face. The look behind her eyes was now more than rage and pain; both were still there, but muted, and along with happiness and love. Her wounds steadily faded into battle scars (much less threatening, but just as sexy). It wasn't long before she started insisting on training again, but after some negotiation, I convinced her to be content with a short walk and shooting some bottles on a fence.

About a month passed. By the standards of the apocalypse, it was a good month. I kind of enjoyed pampering Veronica the way I did, and she in turn grew to like being pampered. Then, one day, the radio the Thaleites gave me buzzed. I flicked it on.

"Sarah Torren? This is Hiru Sanday, Thaleite diplomatic wing." The voice was very matter of fact.

I kept my tone casual. "Hey. What's up?"

"What's Commander Wainwright's condition?"

I glanced over to where Veronica was lounging, idly watching Willow's collection of dated murder mysteries and occasionally mocking them. "Improving. Have you got the latest reports from the doctors?"

"I do. We need her to come back in."

I frowned; Veronica was certainly in much better condition but still not in peak form. "Are you sure? I mean, if it's fate-of-the-world stuff …"

Sanday's tone changed little. "It is. Highest tier of operation."

"I'll put her on," I said reluctantly. I walked over to Veronica and handed her the radio.

She sat up, pausing the TV. "What's up? … Alright, procedure, can I get access codes? … Good. So, docs say I'm good to go? … Understood. Be there soon. Veronica out." She switched off the radio and stood. "Briefing's classified, have to do it in person. I'll let you know what I can afterwards."

I didn't want to see her go. But if the world really did need her, I would just have to hope that she was healed enough to do whatever was deemed necessary. As she passed me, I gently took her hand. "Veronica …" What was there left to say? *Be safe?* She was going into battle. *I love you?* We both already knew that. *I want to see you again?* I'd already said that. All that was left was the feeling. So, I pulled her down into a kiss. We held it for a long while, making the most of the flimsy excuse for her to remain just a few seconds more. Slowly, she pulled away. Slowly, she walked out of the door. Slowly, the door slid shut behind her.

I needed to give myself something to do. So, I started cleaning up. It distracted me for nowhere near long enough. So, I got to making some more protective charms. Unfortunately, I'd run out of materials, and Katey had only just left to scrounge up some more, so she wouldn't be back for a few hours. There wasn't enough food for me to risk our stores by having a snack. So, after tidying what I could of the bunker, I found myself alone with my thoughts. Dark thoughts of emptiness and worry.

When the Thaleite radio buzzed, I leapt to my feet and sprinted over to answer. "Hello?"

"It's me."

"V? What's up?"

Veronica's voice was the dreadful evenness of someone on the precipice. "I'm going after The One. There's a plan, can't tell you. But we're going to kill him. Try, anyhow."

The Thaleites versus … God. Even Veronica knew that this was a long shot. And if she failed … I could only muster a trembling whisper. "Give them hell, honey."

Only a ghost of mirth graced Veronica's voice. "Don't I always?"

Static.

I'd already written a note to Katey saying I'd be out of the bunker for a few hours before I'd even consciously decided where I was going. But I had to watch, in whatever way I could.

I found a scavenger and paid her the last of my charms to get a lift to an observatory on the edge of town. She made one or two attempts at small talk, but I never cared for it at the best of times, to say nothing of now. The climax of the apocalypse, one way or another. Everything else seemed pointless. Even this trip. I just had to try to be as close as I could.

The trip involved a lengthy, winding road up the side of a mountain, which came to an abrupt stop when we encountered a squad of Thaleite guards. They gestured for us to stop, hands on their pistols. When the scavenger did so, one of the guards approached the car window. "Can I ask your business?"

The scavenger jerked a thumb towards me. "Playing taxi for her."

I explained, "My partner, Veronica Wainwright, she's … in the heavens. Literally. I wanted to watch, in whatever way I could."

The guard frowned. "She told you we were here?"

I shook my head. "No, this is just the only place you can really get a view of the heavens, at least with what magic I know."

The guard leaned closer. "You're a mage?"

As I showed him my Circle pendant (not quite as meaningful with the Spire's destruction), I heard Semriel call, "Let the mage through. I know her."

Another guard said, "You're not our commanding officer."

Semriel rolled her eyes. "What are you even protecting? The die's cast. We're marginally improving our crew's chances of getting back *if* they actually win. Which we know is a long shot.

For humanity's sake, let the woman keep an eye on the one she loves."

As the guards considered the situation, the scavenger said, "Look, you tell me to turn around, I'll do it right away. I'll keep my mouth shut. Don't know anything about this, not sure I want to."

The Thaleite squad leader sighed. "Search the mage. I don't want her bringing weapons. The other woman leaves."

As I exited the car, the scavenger asked, "You, uh, got a plan for a ride back?"

"I'll figure something out," I replied, meaning *nothing else matters to me; if something goes wrong, I don't want a way back.*

The guards patted me down, confiscating my pouch of magical reagents for fear I'd cause trouble with them. Semriel then took it from them, grumbling a promise to stop me from causing trouble. Then, she led me further into the observatory. It had been abandoned since the start of the apocalypse—space exploration was evidently not a priority when the dead were rising all around. Near one of the larger telescope domes there was a camp, established for a much larger group than currently occupied it, consisting of Thaleites and a handful of their allies, like werefolk clans and a few fey. I was vaguely reminded of the coalition that had been assembled to assault the Demon Lord, but this was a fraction of the size, in both raw number and the variety of factions represented. Most were milling around aimlessly, anxious as I was for news of the battle beyond. A few were working around a device resembling a large gold and silver gateway, angled slightly forward.

Semriel called to them, "Hey, got room for a mage?"

A wererat carrying a hammer poked his head out from beneath a hatch. "Well, we don't have any right now, so if she's got any ideas … well, we're a little light on those right now."

At the quizzical look I gave her, Semriel explained, "We used that thing to send the strike team to heaven. But it burnt out, meaning they can't use it to get back. Almost moot compared to whether or not they'll take out The One, but on the off chance they pull it off …"

It was something to occupy my mind, at any rate. "I'll see what I can do."

'What I could do' turned out to be not all that much. For a while, my magical expertise brought some new approaches to the repair team, mages being much more scarce after the Spire's destruction, but most led to dead ends. Over time, hopes of repair waned, along with hopes for the strike team. As evening started to fall, more and more agreed that the team couldn't have kept fighting so long. More and more made to leave. When the first stars started appearing in the sky, it was just myself and Semriel. I'd set aside any hopes of repairing the gate to heaven, instead working on enchanting one of the abandoned telescopes so that I might at least see what was happening there. It was harder than I thought, especially with a lack of research material to reference.

Eventually, I allowed myself a break. Semriel and I sat on a small bench, watching the planets slowly float through the void. We were silent for a long time.

Semriel found something to say. "You were everything to her, you know. So much lost in the apocalypse … these days, it's easy to find something to die for. Harder to find something to live for."

"I wish I could have done more."

Semriel gently put an arm around me. "You brought her comfort. You mortals don't value that enough."

"She brought me comfort, as well."

Semriel smiled sadly. "See? Win-win."

"I made a promise to ——" I abruptly stopped talking as I felt something brush over my supernatural senses. Semriel obviously felt something too, as she tensed up.

Then we saw the immense, golden explosion, like a second sun, far above, illuminating the sky as it returned to its rightful blue.

I stood, hope blooming in my heart. "Is that …?"

Semriel laughed. "They did it! Those crazy bastards, they did it!"

I laughed along with her. Now there was a chance Veronica had made it. And even if she hadn't, then her sacrifice had saved the world; my mourning was a small price to pay for humanity's salvation.

Something caught Semriel's attention, and she rushed over to the nearby telescope. "Um … okay, so good news, your girlfriend wasn't killed by The One; bad news, unless you have a very clever idea, she could well be killed by the impact."

I blinked. "The impact with …?" I looked up and saw a number of fragments of angel dust falling towards Earth. Among them, a few humanoids. One particularly large and burly one struggling to slow her fall with an angel's wing.

I didn't have a very clever idea. But I did have a very simple idea, and under the circumstances, it would have to do. I gathered what was left of my magical reagents and started hurriedly etching runes on the ground. I then worked to conjure something very big and very fluffy. It was a large-scale conjuration, but my skills had been refined over the course of the apocalypse, and my magical energy was at full charge. I ended up burying myself in all the fluff, but that wasn't all that important. What was important was keeping the construct intact long enough for Veronica to impact it, hopefully no longer at literally-break-neck speed.

I felt something hit the massive mound of fluff hard, followed by a couple more somethings. Realising that Veronica wasn't alone, I decided to hold the conjuration as long as I could. It was a strain holding something so big in one piece, especially since the construct was such a rush job, but it held long enough for a few more somethings to hit it, before a long pause, after which my grip on the spell finally failed. Still, I seemed to have got everyone.

Including the one that mattered most—to me, anyway. As the fluff faded, I saw Veronica. Her armour had been torn off at some point, leaving only tattered military fatigues. She sported a number of new burns and deep cuts, and she was covered in ash. She was also smiling. She slowly stood, and her smile brightened further as she saw me. She was too exhausted to say anything. There was nothing that needed saying. I rushed towards her. We kissed deeply as the ruins of heaven rained down to Earth around us.

Some would later say that this was the day that everything went back to normal. But 'normal' was gone forever. Everything had changed. Governments and institutions were fractured, and there wasn't anyone alive that wasn't mourning a friend lost in the apocalypse. Many didn't have a home to go back to, and of those that did, many had lost much to rampaging demons or desperate scavengers.

But people started to rebuild. The ashes of the old world proved foundations enough to build something new. For those without homes, new ones were found or built. People began to reorganise, and the disaster brought together disparate groups of people and forged friendships that would last for life. Also, as heartless as it was, at least the massive casualties meant there was more room and food for those that survived.

Many institutions had failed, but humanity was better off without some, and people took the chance to build something better. Groups took over abandoned factories and businesses and turned them into worker co-ops. The supply lines shattered in the apocalypse demanded a sudden shift to renewable forms of power and careful recycling of what people had, and most decided to stay with this new paradigm. Nature started moving back in, and people were more careful with it this time around. A few new governments cropped up in places where the old governments had lost control or collapsed entirely. While not all was good—a few settlements had been conquered by corporations or tyrants—most people were making the best of the new world.

While the supernatural becoming public brought many threats to the fore, it also brought new solutions. The old gods, those benevolent, wicked and all in between, found a whole new generation of followers. The skills of wizards remained in high demand, and despite the shattering of the Circle, it wasn't too hard for one to find an apprentice to pass down their skills (and handle the more tedious parts of magic). Governments, new and old, established new treaties with supernatural factions for trade and protection.

But that would all come much later. For now, I was worried about Veronica. Only a handful of her team had made it back from the assault. The few survivors took it in their stride, more or less. Most had considered the entire affair a suicide mission anyway and had got their affairs in order beforehand. The fact that *anyone* made it back was cause for celebration. Semriel managed to get an abandoned car working, and she drove the strike team to get much-needed medical attention. Veronica accepted it without protest, which made me deeply concerned about how serious her wounds must have been.

Luckily, the doctors assured me that Veronica would make a full recovery. Unfortunately, I couldn't visit her while she was in hospital, as her extensive enhancements required the direct attention of Thaleite doctors, who treated her in a secure facility, but it wasn't long before telecommunications were brought back up, so we could speak every day.

Willow and Katey were able to move back out, so I once again had the bunker to myself. We still spoke regularly, each of us keeping an eye on the others. While I had done what I did for Pat, Willow and Katey were nonetheless incredibly grateful. They were still very much mourning their son and brother, of course, but they still had a life to live.

After a month, Veronica sent word that she was being released from hospital and the bunker was the first place she was heading. I spent the rest of that day hurriedly stocking it with all of her favourite foods and making sure the place was tidy. When she arrived, the first thing we did was undo all the work I'd done in making the bed.

I woke up the next morning to the sensation of Veronica gently stroking my hair. Not having the apocalypse looming over our heads made the moment all the more blissful. More than just reprieve—real rest and relaxation. We'd have plenty more of these moments to look forward to. But this was the first of many, and that made it all the more special. I ended up dozing back off in her embrace.

Eventually, my stomach was insistent enough for breakfast for me to finally get up and answer its demands. As we ate, Veronica decided we should get to catching up. "So, what have you been doing lately?"

"Still selling magic charms, going freelance," I said casually. "It's not much, but it's keeping me fed. Going to be a while before the Circle gets back together, if it ever does."

"Need a new job?" Veronica asked.

I looked up. "You have an idea?"

"Thaleite auxillia. We recruit folks with supernatural powers all the time. Your Circle connections made that kind of awkward beforehand, supernatural politics and all, but now there's no Circle …" Veronica took another bite of her meal.

I considered the idea. "I take it there are non-combat jobs? I'm not you. At all."

Veronica smirked. "Yeah, don't worry. Remember that shield you made me? It kinda burnt out a while back, but with Thaleite backing, you might be able to make more resilient versions. I'm sure I could convince the quartermaster to pay you for a steady supply of those things. Or there's consultant jobs; dealing with magic, we could use someone who knows about it." Then, Veronica grinned. "It'd also get you a room in the barracks. If you wanted."

Well. The bunker wasn't all that comfortable anyway, and proximity to Veronica … As I considered the problem, Veronica switched the subject. "By the way, I'll probably be in and out for a while. Still some asses that need kicking around. I'll help Command pick up the pieces. Once things calm down a little, then I'll … take some leave." She started to tear up.

"Veronica?" I whispered.

To my surprise and relief, she was smiling. "Sorry, it's just …" Suddenly, she stood, walking around to me, picking me up and holding me tightly.

I held her in turn. "Hey, hey. I'm here. Everything's going to be alright, thanks to you."

"I know, I know, and …" She sniffed, struggling to get her words in order. "I'm excited. All this time, all my *life*, I've been fighting. I had a shit father, in a shit town, joined the army to get away, and now … I'm going to have a break. I'm not going to fight. And I'm *looking forward* to it."

I softly caressed her cheek. "Of course you are."

"And it's because of you." She kissed me softly. "Sarah … thank you. Thank you so much."

I really couldn't think of anything to say to that.

A couple of months later, I was on a massive cargo plane, flying in the sky above the Northern Territory. I crouched in a back compartment, marking the armour of Thaleite soldiers with protective runes. I had got into a solid rhythm, marking each soldier's armour before instructing the next to come forward with a gesture.

Veronica walked into the room. "Two minutes to drop, Sarah. You nearly done?"

I glanced at the line. "Just a couple left, honey."

Veronica seemed satisfied and joined the end of the line. I reached her with a bit under 30 seconds to go. When I indicated I had finished, she took the chance to steal a kiss before fastening her respirator. As she moved to the opening exit ramp, I called out, "Kick their asses, honey!" Veronica gave me a thumbs up before leaping out of the plane, her soldiers following her. I moved towards the front of the plane, where the operation's support staff were receiving a feed from the soldiers' body cams. I sat back and watched Veronica work.